The Art Of
Poet Philosopher

The Art Of
Poet Philosopher

CORTEZ BRASEAN

THE ART OF POET PHILOSOPHER

iUniverse books may be ordered through booksellers or by contacting:

iUniverse
1663 Liberty Drive
Bloomington, IN 47403
www.iuniverse.com
1-800-Authors (1-800-288-4677)

ISBN: 978-1-5320-9963-2 (sc)
ISBN: 978-1-5320-9965-6 (hc)
ISBN: 978-1-5320-9964-9 (e)

Library of Congress Control Number: 2020908921

Print information available on the last page.

iUniverse rev. date: 05/21/2020

For the Youth

I would like to say that our youth and children are everything. They need to be taught properly and aided with positivity. For the ones that will take the time to read and comprehend the message in my book. Let my mistakes be something you can learn from. That way while you're learning what could be the best thing you can do. To get through school or accomplish anything you put your mind to. You can also learn what not to do. Allow my words to inspire you to strive for anything you want. Mistakes will be made it's the lessons learned, and the experience gained that we grow from. Even though I started this extradition from a jail cell. All I ever wanted to do was build something we all can be a part of. It's from that jail cell on a modern-day plantation. That I chose to change my way of thinking and do something positive for our youth and families. That righteous mind state dwells within us all. It's up to us as individuals to manifest that construction for correction in our lives. Let me be the one to tell you what they refuse to say. That is you're great and amazing as the creation itself. You're capable of achieving anything that you put your glorious minds to. The world is yours and everything in it is at the tip of your fingers. Always remember to utilize what you know and never abuse it. To my two lovely daughters Lakieya and Riley and my one and only son Elijah. Daddy will always love you to the moon and back. I ask that you forgive your father for my absence in your life and the hardship it has caused. The three of you are my deepest strength and my greatest influence to do something righteous for our futures. I want you all to know and remember me for more that I have displayed in the past. I appreciate and thank everyone who supported and believed in me during my time of confinement. I'm not going to get into naming, you know who you are. This is only the beginning of something greater. All praise to the Most High may peace and blessing be upon us all.

Contents

Revealing of Spoken Words

Short Story 1

No relation regarding anyone outside this
context is intended by the author.

Chapter 1

I rolled over from my slumber almost tripping over my fiancé's three-inch stilettos and make my way to the bathroom. Enjoying my moment of silence and the early morning peace. I sparked the rest of my spliff from the night before. Inhaling the strong aroma chills spread over my body as I continue to stroll through my phone checking all my gadgets. A smile forms on my face, I guess the potent Cali strain is taking affect. Life has been treating me well as I gain a peace of mind in my own home. Breaking my concentration, I hear my fiancé's voice calling my name from the bedroom. I quickly flushed the last of my medication washed my hands, brushed my teeth, and ran a steamy hot rag over my face. Before accompanying my queen in the master bedroom. Morning sweetheart, I say right before pulling back the satin sheets and joining her as we cuddle up. Why didn't you give me some of your medicine daddy? Shanti spoke in a soft seductive tone. It's plenty more where that came from baby plus you know my morning routine. I calmly stated enjoying the silhouette formed across Shanti's body from the light ray penetrating through the window blinds. Yes, I know your routines alright and from the sound of your voice seems as if you're ready for your other morning dosage. Shanti teased. Of course, sweetheart you know you're my strength I whispered planting soft kisses over her neck and earlobe. Enjoying the passion Shanti let out soft moans guiding my head towards her midsection. "So we're having breakfast in bed." I joked while removing her silk thong from beneath her waist. No daddy more like Burger King because you can have it your way. Shanti purred in a more sensational tone. That immediately made my manhood rise from semi to fully loaded. So, I treated myself to a face full of dove chocolate Shanti instantly went from quite polite schoolgirl to countryside wild girl. Rotating her hips back and forth spreading her juices over my lips releasing lite screams from every lick. Shanti was having the ride of her life climaxing to the maximum capacity. Oh my God daddy yes give it to me. Shanti purred! I immediately started rising to the occasion kissing and licking from her belly button and juicy nipples clean her up to her necklace. Climbing in between her legs I gently penetrated her juicy honey pot. Digging deeper and deeper speeding up my stroke with anticipation whole ate the same time gripping her soft thick juicy booty cheeks from the bottom making sure she feels every rhythm in my body. Shanti purred yes daddy, yes ohh, I'm about to oh yes, I love you daddy. Shanti sang into my ears causing me to inject all my protein inside her nectars. I just rested in between her thighs whole she caressed my back, and we shared wet kisses. I go hard for the money. One hundred two hundred. So hard or the money, so hard for the money. Yo Gotti ringtone blazing from my I phone 5c alerted me. See ma you got me dozing off while I'm still inside you. "Well that's what this dove chocolate will do for you Mr. Ahmir", Shanti said. Oh, is that right Mrs. Shanti? "Sho you right daddy", Shanti said playfully. Now who is that calling you this early in the morning anyway? It better not be any of your groupies Ahmir. Come on ma you know I don't give my number out like that. Ahmir stated defensively. If my phone ring you can best believe it's about the money? I have to get up anyway and get ready. I have business to take care of sweetheart. Kissing Shanti's forehead and rolling from between her legs climbing out of the king-sized bed. I almost tripped over the damn stilettos again. "Be careful baby", Shanti said as she was turning over getting comfortable like she was going to get her a little more beauty rest before starting her day. Baby how many times do I have to ask you to place your red bottoms and all your other fancy shoes where they're supposed to go. You not gone be happy until you kill me, I said making my way to the bathroom. Twisting the shower knob to hot I grabbed a dry off towel from the cabinet placed it on the hook and stepped under the jet streams. This is the life I dreamed of I thought as I enjoyed my morning shower. My gorgeous fiancé all our bills are paid, and business is going well. I mean what more can a king ask for. I contemplated in my mind as I finished up my shower. After freshening up and getting dressed. I had a few calls to make. Dig this Chuckee I'm on my way now just make sure I'm next in your chair. I don't have time for Drew or Mike shenanigans today. I need to be in and out like a robbery dig me. Like a shovel big bra, I got one in the chair now that I'm putting the final touches on, stated Chuckee, just come on through and I'm gone work you in. I need to get at you about some business anyway family. Say no more I ended the call grabbed my keys off the counter to my super sport Camaro sparked a spliff and made my way towards Mirror Cutz Barber Shop. No matter what them people say I'm going to love 'you anyway you are my light I can't let go. Even if we fuss and fight try until we get it right you are my light I can't let go. On my grown man campaign, I let Anthony Hamilton blaze the car stereo speakers saucing the vibe to my Saturday morning. I took a few more pulls for the aroma then put it out cracked my windows. Sprayed the baby powder blunt effect trying to kill the smell as I pulled in Mirror Cutz parking lot. Stepping from behind tinted windows of my Camaro feeling sharp as a double-edged razor blade. I hit the speed dial button to Peter Rabbits phone for the third time this morning. Feeling concerned about constantly getting Rabbit's voicemail. This is not like him not answering his phone. I see if it was going straight to voicemail, but it's ringing like nine times before the voicemail activate. This fool tripping, he knows I got to come scoop that cash up this morning. I thought to myself as I hit the end on my iPhone 5C and stepped through the barber and salon doors. What it do family? Mike said as I took my seat in front of Chuckee's booth. Slow motion family everything cop esthetic trying to get a quick touch up before I get on this mission. I can dig it Mike said. Noticing that Chuckee' s client was getting up I sent a quick text to Rabbit' s phone informing him to get at me asap. What's good big bra? Chuckee stated as we embraced one another before I took a seat in his chair. Man, just cooling like a wine cooler I ain't making no noise big bra. "That's exactly what I wanted to rap with you about family." Chuckee said Word around town you got hat real pressure I'm talking gas ninety-three octane premium. So, if you do then you can break me off some for my personal use only. You know I' m gone get you in there like chin hair I already know how you like it fam. Bald taper for the sides and back razor line that joint to make sure it's extra crispy then sauce it up with the black ice. Ahmir nodded with approval check this my guy if you want strong then I got Hercules for you when you done doing your magic. I'm gone make that happen for you. "Say no more." Chuckee said as he adjusted my seat and went to work with his instruments. Dusting the hair from my shoulders and spraying a touch of olive oil sheen on my fresh cut. Chuckee spun me around in the chair and passed me his hand mirror. With a quick glance of the sides and back I admired who I saw in the mirror. Now those are works to a masterpiece they don't call this place Mirror Cutz for nothing I dapped Chuckee and signaled for him to come to my car. In and out like a drive through family that's what I'm talking about because this spot getting packed. I said as Chuckee took his seat on my leather seats. "It's Saturday to I probably won't make it out of here until about six or seven tonight big bra." Chuckee said with excitement knowing that will be a good pay day for him. "Get that cash flow bro you know the code we live by." I said adjusting the controls to the a.c in my coupe. "By any means I truly appreciate you filling this prescription for me also. I have a date tonight and I'm thinking about dressing up and going to N.A.S.A." stated Chuckee with sarcasm in his voice. "Well that's gone do it for you my guy." I said laughing with sarcasm in my voice. With a quick dap and fair well Chuckee raised from the leather bucket seats of the super sport Camaro and went back to work.

Chapter 2

Contemplating on my next move I switched the five-disc cd changer to Luca Brasi sparked the rest of the spliff and gathered my thoughts. Enjoying the a.c I was strolling through my phone thinking that this is nothing like Perter Rabbits to not call or text. So, I speed dialed Rabbit for the sixth time today. "What' s up what's up?" Rabbit answered with excitement in his voice. Bring it down a notch jack in the box. I been trying to reach you all day and you mean to tell me you not gone hit back at all. "I don't know what you smoking that got you all dysfunctional, but you need to put it out because we got business to take care of just in case it slipped your mind genius." I calmly stated before taking a pull and inhaling the medicated strain into my lungs. "Now, Now pimping I just got caught up with his mad freak from the club 731 last night. I'm talking baby girl doing three sixty and all." Rabbit said sounding like a kid in the candy store. "Well congratulations Romeo you just made the top of my shit list. Now put on your 3d glasses because I' m headed straight at you. I'm coming to scoop that cash up like pronto so be ready." I said feeling irritated as I ended the call, putting the whip on reverse and screeched out of Mirror Cutz parking lot. Fifteen minutes later I was parking outside of Rabbit's apartment complex. Taking a photo graphic mental note of the pink and white two door Beemer Coupe. Sitting pretty with 20-inch Furgiauto's on Perrelli tires. Parked next to Rabbit's fully loaded limited edition Z71 Tahoe. My first thought was maybe Rabbit him a snow bunny. Then again, he not dripping that much sauce to pursue any woman in her right mind. Especially one who drives a car as fly as mine to spend the night with him. The thought faded as I laughed it off exiting my vehicle making my way up the flight of stairs to Rabbit's doorstep. "It's probably one of his neighbor's guest." I said aloud before ringing the doorbell. "It's open." a voice yelled from the other side of the door. "Bless this house." I stated upon entering the luxurious apartment. Well put together might I add, "I like what you're doing with the pad. Now where that receipt at? I can't stay long." "It's in that Loui nap sack right there." Rabbit said, grabbing three shot glasses and a bottle of 1800 tequila, my favorite. From his miniature bar has setup across one of the kitchen counters. "So, this the whole twenty-seven thousand, or do I have to count it?" I asked opening the designer bag observing the neatly stacked big faced bills separated in rubber band stacks. Be my guest doctor you can count it and take a couple of shots with me and Snow Cone before you race up out of here. "Snow Cone, who is Snow Cone?" I asked with curiosity never taking my eyes off the paper stacks. "Aubrey!" Rabbit yelled towards the back of his apartment. Would you mind joining me in the living room? I have someone I want you to meet. Within a matter of seconds Aubrey come strutting through the living room greeting me with a handshake and smile. Wearing nothing but a Golden State Warriors basketball jersey. I couldn't help noticing all of her feminine features. She stood five for five inches about one hundred fifty pounds curvy hips, tight waist, shoulder length curly blonde hair, dark green eyes, and popping pink lips. "Aubrey meet Ahmir, and Ahmir this is Aubrey my personal assistant." Rabbit said with a smirk on his face. I extended my hand, "Nice to meet you Ms. Aubrey." The pleasure is all mine Mr. Ahmir. We shook hands then Aubrey grabbed a seat next to Rabbit on the sofa. With a quick three-way toast, I knocked the shot back and placed the shot glass back on the table. "Pour me up one more Rabbit, I need one to go before I go on this mission. "Not a problem big bra knock yourself out and enjoy it." Rabbit stated. Look here Rabbit I'm going to meet Hunnit and handle the business. Just as soon as I'm done, and I get to a designated area I'm gone hit your line. So, you and Snow Cone keep an ear out for me please. I need you on full alert until I give you the green light that the mission is complete. Shaking off the bum from the tequila running through my body. It was obvious how distracted my man was, all his attention was on Aubrey. She was a stone-cold freak for real. Snow Cone had completely straddled Rabbit's lap and he had her breast out. Doing what sounded like the motorboat right in front of me, as if I wasn't in the room. All I could see was Aubrey's pretty, round firm butt cheeks sticking out from underneath the basketball jersey. Feeling a little agitated I snatched up the Loui bag filled with currency and headed for the door. "Just pick up you phone my love." I said before exiting the apartment. Deep down I was happy for my man and I couldn't blame him. You only get one life to live, and with a freak spontaneous freak like Snow Cone Rabbit most definitely had his hands full. At least he didn't forget about the business he had the cash on point like a true boss. From the looks of it Aubrey just might be the diamond in the dirt that Rabbit had been searching for. She had to be papered up with them fly ass wheels on her luxury coupe. I thought to myself as I let the engine roar in the parking lot. Sitting behind tinted windows I twisted up the medicated strain in a leaf. I took a few pulls from the spliff and let the herb ease my nerves. Contemplating on the task at hand. I suddenly got a suspicious feeling about what was about to happen next.

Brushing it off I didn't sweat it maybe it was the paranoia maybe it was just from the herb or maybe instincts. Either way I had unfinished business to tend to and that was my objective. The quicker I get it done the quicker I can get to my comfort zone. Girl I wish that I could spend time with you each and every day. Praying on my emotions that's the thing that has me open and I don't know what to do to let you know you're my girl to let you know you' re my bae bae. Sammie, "I like love" song blazed my phone alerting it was my considerate fiancé. I knew it was her because I had her number programed to that song specifically. What up ma? Hey daddy! How's everything going I instantly gained strength from the sound of Shanti's voice. Everything going steady love, I' m getting ready to wrap things up now. When I'm done in about another hour, we can go have lunch or whatever you like ma. Well Mr. It sounds like a date. Just call me when you're done. I'm going to stop by my mom's house and let her talk my ears off. So, when you finish up, I will be waiting for you. I'm gone come scoop you ma soon as I'm done. Ok daddy I love you. Love you too ma. Ending the phone call. I started scanning the audio system for some traveling music. Adjusting the controls to Rap and Hip Hop, I put the coupe in drive and started to navigate the streets. Eleven forty-seven a.m. the digital clock read I was making perfect time and determined to finish like a champion. Then accompanying my fiancé for a relaxing lunch. Sticking to what I thought was the master plan I made my wat towards the Grove approximately thirty minutes away.

Chapter 3

Now Mr. One Hunnit was an old school type cat, but he wasn't old. One Hunnit couldn't have been no older than his early forties. More likely he spent thirty of those years molding his life into what it consists of now. You know Mauri Gators, Tom Ford suit wearing guy. He always kept a clean cut and he was a fast talker real smooth operator. Just judging by his appearance, you would have never mistaken him for a person who is a part of the drug trade. I hate to admit it, but he was, and he had mob ties also. He was like a modem day Raffel Edmonds just exclude the flashy jewelry and reckless acts. Mr. One Hunnit was Atlantic Ocean deep in the game, and I had been rocking with him for the last three years. He always gave me the green light whenever I wanted to roll, so I had the upmost respect for him. All I had to do was put the cash for whatever I wanted to get in his hands then he would take care of the rest. Like I said we had been rocking for the last three years so the bond was substantial. Mr. One Hunnit was worth at least seven or right figures so I hardly ever worried about him playing money games with my paper. The setup we had orchestrated was perfect and we ran with it like clockwork every Saturday. One Hunnit was programmed like dish network and his words were law. So, when he said something nine times out of ten it was true, he did it or it was about to happen. My biggest concern was keeping my end of the bargain. Long as Rabbit completed any obstacle, I gave him then we were on deck, everything else was a go. Today was just like any other Saturday and I was making perfect timing. I had the cash in a Louis bag, and I was about five minutes away from the Grove. I sent a quick text to Hunnit informing him that I was about to pull up with the newspaper. Newspaper was a parable or code for cash and that's how we communicated. Now Hunnit was very preserved he didn't drink or smoke so I knew this would be fast. I was gone be in and out like a robberyn then I was off to scoop my wifey for lunch. Realizing I haven't eaten all morning really made me hungry and in need of a hot meal. Pulling in front of Mr. One Hunnit building, I didn't even pay attention to all the new model cars parked on the lot. This was an upscale complex. Everything looked normal so I just grabbed the bag full of cash and headed up the stairway. I knocked on the door three times signaling that it was me then waited for him to let me in. As the door opened, I was greeted with a gun and police badge to my face. Then from behind four more drug task force agents ambushed me screaming "freeze get down on the ground police!" I instantly surrendered putting my hands up dropping to the ground, not wanting to get shot by the crooked cops. More concerned about my safety than anything with all these barrels pointing to my wig. I wasn't worried about nothing I had done because all I had on me was cash. Once I was detained, they rushed me into the apartment. What I saw next caught me by complete surprise two henchman had my guy hog tied to a chair. These weren't the average stick up kids. These two cats were short stocky with silk black hair. They had to have been from one of them foreign cartels or something. "Looks like you're just in time for the party solider we were expecting you." One of the policemen stated in a raspy tone. "What the fuck are you doing to my guy?" I exclaimed with rage in my voice. They had Mr. One Hunnit butt naked with serve cuts and bums all over his body. It looked like one of his eyes had been burned out. His body was completely lifeless. Calm down lil tiger." the same policeman spoke up." No one else said a word, but I could hear voices coming from their radios. It was a different language, so I assumed it was Spanish. "So, what are y' all cooked cops trying to take my man for all he got?" I stated with no sign of fear. No sir young tiger we're not cops at all, you just got yourself caught between Vernon Hills crossroads. The creepy cop or fake cop continued to speak. Now you may know Vernon as a good friend which I can't blame you for. Vernon has done some very treacherous things and that's why we are here to remind him who's in command. We got what we came for so if you want to walk out of here alive today then there are a few rules I must bring to your attention. Right then and there I knew my life would change drastically. I guess the grim reaper was here to make his judgment on me and One Hunnit lifestyle. My stomach felt weaker and weaker, but I didn't show any signs of weakness as the man gave me the run down on our whole operation. He even called my government name informing me about my fiancé where we lived and everything, the whole hundred yards. Now if you decide to walk out of here today then its guidelines you must abide by. The guy continued to speak making my stomach do summer saults. So, what you witnessed today you didn't see at all. Plus, that bag you got wrapped around your neck there take and a reward along with your life. Now, you're free to leave at your own risk just remember I have eyes everywhere and I will be checking on you. I got up from my knees and took one last look at what was left of a true mentor in my life. Without saying a word, I made eye contact with all seven faces in the room. Getting a photo graphic memory of the redemption I just lived then exited the building. Before getting in my car I took a quick glance at the newer modeled cars parked in the lot. I could make out body figures in at least three of the vehicles and they were looking directly at me from behind tinted windows. Without hesitation I got into my car and raced toward my mother-in-law's house. My thought process was on ten I couldn't believe what had just taken place. Knowing that this would be something I would take to my grave. I had a hard time dissecting everything. Damn, Mr. One Hunnit was too sharp for his own good. I guess these folks don't be who they say they are.

I couldn't make it to my fiancé quick enough it felt like I had been driving for hours. Every intersection I was pulling into was catching red lights and it seemed as if all the cars were following me. When I finally reached my mother-in-law's house I just parked and said a deep prayer. Shanti was headed my way with a big smile on her pretty face. I hit the unlock switch so she could get in. She hopped in kissed the side of my face and said she wanted Applebee' s. "Is everything of baby?" Shanti asked. Yes ma, just a little exhausted and ready to eat. I need you to do me one more favor sweetheart. What's that daddy? Drive us there baby I need to relax a little bit. No problem daddy. As I was getting in Shanti was climbing over to the driver seat. I buckled my seatbelt reclined my seat and laid-back gaining composure. I tried to block out what I just witnessed. Shanti adjusted her seat put on some slow jams and she sang and hummed all the way to the restaurant. Feeling so blessed and grateful to be in my lady's presence all I could do was give praise and thanks to the Most High. We placed our orders and we waited. I have a confession to make Shanti. I think it's time for a change I'm ready to switch the game up ma. Remember all that writing I was doing when I was incarcerated. Yes, I do baby. Well I think it's time to put that in motion. Even if don't gain success off my works, my biggest goal is to inspire someone. I just want to live more righteously ma. If anything, happens to me, I want to leave something behind in good remembrance of me you know. I want to get real creative with it, do something different and put a book together. Create a person of character add a life experience based on a true story that will lead up to the revealing of a mindset and a new way of thinking the philosophies. What you think ma? "You know I been trying to get you to pursue that, Daddy. I told you that you're a great writer. I still have all of your love notes that you wrote me when you were away." "Well say no more, my love. Let's enjoys our meal and when we get home, I have a surprise for you.". Shanti just smiled from ear to ear symbolizing her satisfaction in her future husband.

Up next the revealing of the philosophies by Philosopher himself. Journey into the mind of one man who was once corrupted by life itself. Experience brought forth understanding and a dream was produced. With strength and power in words my mission is to inspire all readers.

Philosophy 1

As I take my time to recollect and redirect my motives, I'm singled handled revealing what has been concealed is now unfolding. Truth separates light from darkness millions of eyes are open, but they're only a few that can see. What can be proved and what is hidden. What should be considered and what is unforbidden. When greatness is demanded, foolishness is not tolerated. We learn from our mistake we grow stronger from our heartbreaks. Disregard simple talk and one-track minds. Burdens will be lifted in due time. Deception has plagued our nations and lead them astray. Abate the duplicity and grasp hold and protect your integrity. Envious and jealous ways are the hand of the wicked. A fool will return to his family and out of his mouth comes nothing worth listening. We seek and strive for perfection and when correction is accepted, we mold and wield paths for what is predestined.

Philosophy 2

The relaxation from meditation soaking up all the thoughts in the world. Risen to higher levels of consciousness at the same time battling emotions and desires. The different drives and urges pretending to be my friend, pretending to be one with me. With them all sharing something in common, but not necessarily understanding the motive. The will the ambition demands truth, progress and positivity. We need consistency and proficient activity on your character means more to me. Let's focus on our tool, sense of responsibility, and quality over quantity. We can make history overcoming our difficulties now that's a real victory.

Philosophy 3

Life can be unpredictable, emotions are so powerful, temptation can sometimes be undeniable. It's easier to hold on than let go even when it's not beneficial. It's times when we make excuses for the ones, we love the most. Sad to say that they're actions show how much they are unreliable. No one is to blame when someone who claims to be a significant other goes against the grain. Just another lesson learned, and another chapter closed because the tables always turn. One man's loss is potentially another man's treasure. For the ones who have been taken for granted don't panic we all lack some knowledge and understanding. Keep in mind all that looks good isn't always so pleasant. Everything that goes up must come down, but every ending doesn't have to be drastic.

Philosophy 4

The mind wonders how growth and satisfaction comes from true love. Wisdom and courage the comfort feeling of being protected. With so many qualities this trait share. Anyone may speak their opinion on this topic. One may agree to disagree, but it's truly an experience that one must live through to know the feeling. A wise man once stated, "What's understood doesn't have to be explained.", but how many hearts cry out for an explanation? Why the pain from an emotional rollercoaster corrupts the mind mentally, and affects the body physically? Why does love sometimes hurt, and how would you know if the love is true or genuine? The same things that makes you laugh can make you cry. Understanding is the virtue risen to elements and learning from what we go through.

Philosophy 5

Consider making wise decisions for you will have to reap the consequences for your actions. Be mindful of the company you keep for evil company corrupts good character. Love yourself for who you are it's not promised that an individual will do the same. Strive for greatness no matter how many times you lose focus. Lost opportunities are symbolic to forgotten destinies know that if can endure it you can pursue it. Composure is key because difficulties are at the hands of the free. Distractions hinder true success while knowledge comes with overcoming distress. Out of silence comes peace while violence brings forth grief. Create happiness don't chase it time should be valued and never wasted.

Philosophy 6

Our toughest battles we struggle with comes from within. At combat between psychological warfare fighting for justice. Understanding gets demanded a product of what has plagued our thought process. Educated with misplaced hatred amongst races and nations who are predestined to fulfill obligations that are far above and beyond simple things which are still basic. Modem day plantations keep us stuck in our own ways, divided lacking knowledge of who and what we are? A message is the only option whether they take heed of imitators or imposters. Preacher man forgive, but I'm the philosopher creating obstacles for the ones who have been deceived. Suffering from an internal mental bleed. Freedom, Justice, Equality is what we believe we deserve. Truth is the avenue rather segregated or subdued we strive until we all rule.

Philosophy 7

We must compromise with ourselves, our families and our culture. Bring peace to the communities and build paths that are based on righteousness. Come together with strength in numbers. There is no greater occupation in the world than to assist another human being to help someone else succeed. We as people must improvise and produce in a way that is historical and everlasting for the ones to come after us. Living in truth and honor for the works we bring into manifestation. Unity will be our key to abate the violence and reckless acts in the neighborhoods. Once we stand for ourselves as individuals then we can stand for one another as a movement and voice for a nation.

Philosophy 8

Words of motivation and inspiration will encourage us to face our fears. Confidence is built from pain and struggle. You capitalize on your weakness and strength. Learning to control what you were once controlled with. Our greatest battles are the ones within our own minds. Overcoming difficulties is what develops good character. Building human potential comes with hard work and determination. The proper knowledge and teachings will replenish the mind and heal in areas we have been deceived. Rational thinking is only the beginning when it comes to building bridges. So, that endeavors correspond with mental attitudes.

Philosophy 9

Hostility lives in the heart of the wicked. Love is the highest form of gratitude and admiration. Time heals all wounds and barriers with time comes true discipline. If you are patient in one moment of anger you can prevent a thousand days of sorrow. We strive to work through conflict and not against it. Understanding where we may have gone wrong and accepting our faults for the choices we make. We make sacrifices for the ones we love and draw strength from the ones we love. True love will not hurt you, but it will deprive poisonous traits that blocks that avenue. Misplaced hatred destroys from within, so we grow to love our family and friends.

Short Story 2

No relation regarding anyone outside this
context is intended by the author.

Chapter 1

It was five minutes before my shift was over, and I was ready to roll. I didn't have to much planned, but I was definitely hitting the town tonight. "Hey, what's up sexy? Slow down and come bless me with your presence." I said trying to gain the attention of the bright yellow petite lady. We were clocking out from work and making our way to the parking lot, but she was moving fast. Slow down beautiful I'm going to make you my wife, you just don't know it yet.

"Excuse me I don't mean to be rude, but you don't know me like that dude." The cute young lady stated in a sassy tone. Forgive me sunshine I didn't mean any disrespect; I just couldn't' let you get away from me today without introducing myself. They call me Ceasar, and do you mind if I get your name. Well my parents named me Amari, and what do you mean you couldn't let me get away from you today? So, you be stalking me or nah? Of course not, your ass not that fine, I just know greatness when I see it. Amari jaw dropped she couldn't believe what this fool just said. I was wondering if you would be interested in allowing me to take you out for a good time. It would be my pleasure getting to know you outside of the work environment. "Pump your breaks Romeo, how do you know if I have a man or not.", Amari said in a sarcastic manner with her hand on her hip. Well correct me if I was wrong Ms. Amari, but the two of us are still young and have our whole life ahead of us. I'm here to remind you that you can always explore your options. Now if you're in a committed relationship then I understand and respect your wishes. "I'm not trying to come in between a happy home." I stated licking my lips with a grin on my face. Ok prince charming it seems as if someone taught you properly but are you sure you want to be seen with a woman like me. You know my ass not that fine remember. Look here sunshine you have natural beauty and that was a joke. I was just being myself I have no hidden agendas. If it's anything that I want from you I will be the first to inform you. All I'm asking from you is to get to know you better under better circumstances. A walk in the park, maybe candle lit dinner, it's whatever you like. "Well Shakespeare since your pouring your heart out I guess you deserve a shot." Amari stated with her cheeks blushing knowing she was feeling the game Ceasar was kicking. Give me your phone so I can put it in sir, then you may call or text me and figure something out. I was smiling ear to ear like a kid in a candy store as Amari programmed her number in my phone. "Well I must go Mr. Ceasar it was nice meeting you make sure you use my number wisely." Amari said as she made her way towards her car. "The pleasure is all mine beautiful and please believe I will use this number to the best of my ability." I stated feeling like mac daddy of the year. "Make sure you drive safe Amari." I yelled out across the parking lot as I made my way towards my vehicle. Climbing into the 4 door 2014 Dodge Ram pick-up with the Hemi VS under the hood and the tomato soup factory paint job. I was feeling like a winner as I brought the engine to life. I thought to myself as I strolled through my playlist checking for some riding music. "Started off with peanuts young street dreamer feeling like Ace Boogie when he first quit the cleaners. I'm gone shock the world Muhammad Ali em.", I let rapper Doe B blaze the woofers as I skirted off the parking lot chucking the deuces at the company security guard. Hungry as a hostage I pulled into the Taco Bell drive thru. "May I take your order?" a voice sounded over the intercom. Yes, I would like a number 8 with extra tomatoes, and a fruit punch Hi-C. Okay sir will you pull to the window for your total, thank you. $7.93 is your total sir would you like some sauce with your order. Yes, hot and mild if you don't mind, and can you put some napkins in there for me. I said as I thumbed through the bank roll looking for a ten dollar bill to pay for my food and drink. I skated off heading towards my apartment thinking to myself that O would stop by the convenient store next to my crib. Knowing I was gone need a couple boxes of optimoes for tonight. You used to call me on my cell phone, light night when you need my love, and I know when that hotline bling that can only mean one thing ever since I left the city girl you. Drake was slapping the subwoofers as I pulled into the store. I have to admit I was amped up it was Friday night I had the weekend off and a pocket full of cash. Let's just say it was party time I hopped out the truck flexing. Trying to make this snappy I went inside the store grabbed a twenty-four oz Bud light platinum two boxes of optimoes paid the clerk then I was out of there with the quickness. When I made it home, I was surprised to see my brother Ahmir Camero sitting in the parking lot. Aww yeah, it's going down I know he got pressure with him. "I thought I was gone have to chase you down." I said out loud as I backed in the parking lot space right next to the super sport Camero. Ahmir and I had a two-bedroom two full bath apartment on the out skirts outside the city limits. It was ducked off and super low key only a handful of people knew we lived there and that's how we kept it. I grabbed my bags hopped out the truck hit the lock switch and went into the building. Our apartment was the first one to the right I put my key in and twisted the locks. Upon entering the living room, I could smell the aroma in the air. Locking the door behind me I went into the kitchen to eat my burritos. I could hear music coming from Ahmir's bedroom, so I knew he had company and didn't hear me come in. Trying to be nosey I crept through the hallway and placed my ear to the door. I could hear moans and screams over the music feeling aroused I had to move around before he cause me eavesdropping. I went back into the kitchen to finish my meal. Once I was done, I went into my bedroom popped the seal on my brewsky then fumbled through my closet for something to sport tonight. I was falling up in somebody club tonight, so I had to be spotlight, camera, action ready. I had two brand new designer outfits that Ahmir bought me from Saks Fifth in Atlanta a couple of weeks ago. I've been waiting patiently for the perfect time to bring em out and sauced up. Just as I was finishing my beverage and putting the final touches to my gear Ahmir bedroom door swung open and he came out butt naked. He had to be high out his mind because he walked straight into my room with a spliff in his mouth trying to pass it to me. The moment I gave him a look like fool is you crazy I assumed he realized he was naked. He just started laughing and ran back in his room. "That guy to damn comfortable." I said aloud as I inhaled the sess into my lungs then holding it for a few seconds. Well hey that's my brother we grew up together so that;s not the first time I saw him naked. Ahmir came back into my room with his shorts and shoes on strolling through his phone. "What's good Ceasar?" he said grinning as I passed the Cali strain back to him and he took a seat at the foot of my bed. Just cooling it home slice. Who the new booty that got you running up in my room with hard on's like that? We just laughed and he started coughing getting choked from the smoke. That's ain't no new booty bro that's Shanti she in the shower now. I see you pulling the Gucci out what's the occasion you must got some new booty you trying to pursue? I guess I'm just feeling myself big bra I want to tum up one tome ya know, but I need you to step out with me family. "Well I didn't have nothing spectacular planned plus Shanti was speaking the same language your talking right now so I guess we can shake some.", Ahmir stated with a mellow tone in his voice. Matter of fact that reminds me I finally got on with that sexy ass red bone from work. I been telling you about. I'm gone shoot her a text and see if she wants to be my Cinderella tonight cause we about to have a ball. Shanti walked into the room and sat on Ahmir's lap giving him sloppy wet kisses. Ahmir tried to come up for a breath, come on ma are you gone at least speak. Laughing out loud Shanti spoke up in a sexy seductive tone. "Hey, Ceasar how was work?" "What's up Shanti? Work was aight you know another day another dollar." I said before passing her the medicated strain. If the two of you not obsessively in love with each other then I don't know what to call it. The three of us just laughed and Shanti kissed Ahmir again before passing him the spliff. I remember when Ahmir came home and got back in touch with you. That boy talked about you all day every day I haven't ever seen him so into a woman like that before. I'm shocked that I don't have any nieces or nephews running around here. Yet, Shanti cut in because this man shoots to kill, I might be pregnant with twins as we speak. Laughing out loud Ahmir just shook his head from side to side. Shanti noticed the designer outfit and all white foams. Okay, Ceasar you about to jump fresh ain't you. So, what are we doing tonight? I got an all-white Prada dress that I'm gone squeeze my sexy ass into and step out to show all these amateur chicks how to put on. Shanti was most definitely feeling the vibe she was smacking her gums and turning up for the occasion. Oh, baby you can wear that all white Givenchy outfit you have with your all white low top number one Jordan's. They gone swear up and down we just stepped off the runway or a magazine. Hold up hold that thought i cut Shanti off she just texted back and said she wouldn't mind spending time. It's about to go down, it's about to go down Ceasar was bouncing off the walls like he hit the lottery. "Who is she?" Shanti asked Ahmir with curiosity in her eyes. Excuse me Ceasar interrupted. I am standing here, and she is the lovely lady that will be accompanying us tonight. Let's just say this collaboration has turned into a double date. It's time to rock steady the night still young now if I'm lucky and play my cards right then Amari shall be filled with cum. Laughing out loud Shanti grabbed Ahmir's hand then guided him towards his bedroom. The two of you need to be handling business and not getting busy, why ya'll creeping off we are going live tonight, and I don't want any excuses. I saw the look in my brother eyes not to mention the way Shanti like to love on him. That guy will lock himself in a room with that woman and I might not see him for days. Now that I think about it I need to give Amari a courtesy call to make sure she on point for the night.

Chapter 2

Who else am I going to lean on when times get rough? Who else gone talk to me on the phone until the sun comes up? Oh, baby baby we belong together. She got Mariah Carey on the ring back tone the limits women will go express their inner feelings. If I wasn't mistaken, I would have thought that song was for me. Let me snap out of it I haven't had the woman number twenty-four hours and I'm already in my feelings. Maybe I'm high whatever it is I know I need to get my life. Hello, a soft voice with such passion in it broke my reverie. Yes, may I speak with Amari. This is she! How are you doing Amari, this is Ceasar. I know who you are Ceasar so what's up? I was just calling to inform you more on what our night consists of. Once again might I thank you for your blessing of being my Cinderella tonight because we are getting ready to have a ball. "I hear you." Amari said popping her lips. Check this my brother and his fiance gone double date and we are all wearing white. I was wondering if that's too much for you, if so then I can switch it up and wear whatever color you are wearing so that I can co-adjust with your situation. I hope I'm not doing too much baby girl; I just want to be on point with you.

Teamwork make the dream work. You're doing fine Ceasar you really made my night better I was thinking about wearing white myself. To be completely honest with you I'm not in the mood for driving tonight and I don't want you to be late picking me up. Dig this baby girl I got you take your time and tum your sexy up a notch. Text me the address where to pick you up from and I will be through to scoop you between 10:30 pm and 11:00 pm if that's suitable for you Ms. Amari. Yes, that's good timing Ceasar. Just text my phone when you are pulling up and I will be ready for you. Say no more baby girl I got you let me sharpen up a little but then we gone make that happen. "Ok see you soon." Amari stated sounding excited. "Believe that." I said before ending that call. With no hesitation I put my phone on the charger connected my Bluetooth to the stereo sync media and let Spotify blaze the speakers. Lil Wayne radio station will get the job done every time. Looking in the mirror I realized that I didn't get me a fresh cut. It's all good I'm the man that's in demand so I gotta turn a trick of the trade. I grabbed the trimmers from the cabinet and went to work. Knocking off all the wild hairs on my face then touching up my line with a razor-sharp edge. I was back like cooked crack in a matter of minutes. Now that's artwork I should be Ebony man of the money I said while laughing to myself. Within twenty minutes I was in and out of the shower smelling fresher than a newborn baby. Glancing at the time I had a little over one hour before I had to pick Amari up. I was making perfect time I thought as I fumbled through my drawer picking out a pair of Polo socks and boxers to comfort me through the night. It may not mean anything to ya' ll, but understand nothing was done for me. So, I don't plan on stopping at all I want this shit forever mane. Lil Wayne ft. Drake, Kanye West, and Eminem want this forever song was pumping the stereo surround sound I had set up in my bedroom. Sliding into my designer Gucci pant with the Gucci belt to match I knew tonight would be a light show. I stepped into my size eleven all white foams then adjusted a few of my pieces the 14 karat gold Cuban links around my neck. I knew my jewelry needed no introduction.

The shower killed my buzz and Amari had me amped up. I knew I would need some Kush to keep this party going until I tap out. Tonight, or in the morning which ever one it maybe I was gone make sire and get the job done. I grabbed the roll of cash from my other pant pocket and pulled off a hundred-dollar bill. I know my brother gone put it in the air, but I need something personal, so I knocked on Ahmir door. Shanti opened the door and passed me the rest of the spliff they were burning. Girl you were reading my mind I'm trying to get on my level. Shanti shook her head laughing then went back in my brother bathroom. "What's good bra?" "I see what you done swagged up and got the Cuban links dancing on your chest I see you family.", said Ahmir with chinky eyes and a huge smile on his face symbolizing that he was most definitely on his level. "I'm trying to get like you bro.", I said passing him the hundred-dollar bill. Serve me proper bro you know how I do my night just might get exquisite and I'm trying to make sure I'm prepared ya dig. "I can dig it big bro you know I got you." said Ahmir as he reached inside the zip lock bag grabbing a handful of the potent Cali strain and putting it in my hand. Appreciate it bra you know I got a couple boxes of optimoes in there if you need any. Most definitely bring me two of em I'm gone twist up now before we leave, and I don't have any more sandwich bags either said Ahmir. Okay bet I got some sandwich bags in my room foo you can get those. Cool my white boy want a zip he is getting ready to pull up. Once I get him out the way I'm gone close shop for the night then we can do us. Say no more bro I went into my room and got the bags for Ahmir. Before I started putting the final touches on my gear, I pearled another spliff then put it rotation with Shanti and Ahmir. That's the way we roll anytime you around is please believe it's a smoke session in progress. They were just about ready to get this ball rolling also. I finished adjusting my collar so that the Cuban links swung properly when I walked. With one last look in the standup mirror I topped it off with a few sprays ofmy Tom Ford cologne. You know what they say when you look good you feel good. I was definitely feeling presidential and with my comrades by my side I was ready to move like a coupe through traffic. I turned off my stereo and grabbed the rest of my accessories the hollered for Shanti and Ahmir to hurry up. I had thirty minutes before picking up Amari. I see the two of you looking good like a modern-day Bonnie and Clyde. Cool, cool it's about that time so Shanti gone and finish popping that lip gloss. Ahmir I need you to grab that Luca Brasi 2 cd out your coupe we are riding Hemi tonight. I want to hear some gansta music we can play that and let it ride remember to lock the door I'm gone be waiting in the truck. I was anxious to pick up Amari so whole waiting in the truck for them to come out I sent her a text letting her know I was on my way. The address she sent was in the city limits and fifteen minutes away. Damn was all I could say when Shanti came strutting down the small flight of steps in front of our complex. Her peanut butter brown skin complexion complemented her pearly white smile and glowing brown eyes. She was slim around the waist area thick in the thighs and backside she had to have double D cups plus she was a ten in the face. The all-white Prada dress she was sporting hugged her curves perfectly she stood no more than five feet seven inches and walked with authority. She looked more stunning than any other runway model. Woman you are wearing that dress was all I could say as she climbed into the backseat. Laughing out loud Shanti responded, "I do this for real these amateur chicks counterfeit." We just laughed as Ahmir was coming out of the building looking like new money. He was puffing on a fresh rolled spliff heading to his coupe to get the cd I requested. I promise this guy was so swavey it was just ridiculous I mean real trendsetter. He wasn't the flamboyant type, but when he steps the guy be dripping so much sauce. He was draped in diamonds and gold like the modern-day pharaoh. He was rocking two chains one platinum chain with white diamonds implanted across the ankh charm, the other gold chain with yellow diamonds implanted across the ankh charm. The all gold Bulova was wrapped around his wrist and every time the light hit him, he looked like a disco ball. Ahmir was clean cut with a chocolate skinned complexion his five nine stocky frame, put you in the mind of a professional boxer. He and Shanti reminded me of Omar Epps and Sanaa Lathan from Love and Basketball. Ahmir hopped in the passenger seat then passed me the sess he popped in the cd and started adjusting his seat. I took a few more pulls from the aroma and held it before passing it to Shanti. After I exhaled it was a moment of silence, and all I could say was I love you man. We all just looked at one another and then burst out into laughter. "You better put this spaceship in drive before you be late picking up your date." said Ahmir trying not to get sentimental with me. I did just that shifted the Hemi in drive and burnt rubber out the complex.

Chapter 3

As I navigated the street, I could tell we was feeling the vibe bobbing to the beat and enjoying the session. "My daily conversation it consists of hustle, it consists of hustle grinded from the bottom sick and tired of struggle police is harassing don't want to see us come up. Word around town they gone check the move, word around town I flex my neck with jewels, word around town me and yo dixie cool and if you broke you know damn well I can't stand next to you.", Kevin Gates blazed the amplifier. I sent Amari a quick text informing her that I would be pulling up less than five minutes. Pulling onto Booker Street a fancy subdivision I turned down the volume, cracked the sunroof and sprayed the baby powder blunt effect. Not wanting to make a bad impression let alone scare the pretty lady off. I just wanted to play it cool so I informed Shanti and Ahmir to feel her out and make sure she can dwell amongst ganstas. Now Shanti was my sister she was like family not to mention she was a rider and thoroughbred. Shanti is perfect for my brother plus I have seen her in action, so I know she solid. She will put me on game if there is any negative or shady energy from Amari so tonight will be interesting. We sat there for like five minutes in complete silence high out our mind. Waiting for one of them to break the ice and say something because I was feeling fishy, she didn't text me back or nothing. Ahmir spoke up are you sure we at the right spot this place is upscale? Not trying to dis you or nothing bro, but I didn't know Duro bags was paying that good. Whoever living up in there gotta be papered up that's six figured home or better. Come Monday morning I'm putting my application in a.s.a.p. real talk. We all laughed, and I strolled through my text messages to make sure. Yea bra this the address she sent me 123 Booker Street. "Well damn Ceasar." Shanti interrupted you scored this time that's a bad ass chick I see coming down the driveway. Ahmir and

I turned or heads like we had whiplash. I was caught in a trance Amari was so damn gorgeous with her bright skin complexion, hazel brown eyes and perky pink lips. Amari stood no more than five feet five inches and possess a petite physique. She had on an all-white Jimmy Choo two piece with the lower part of her belly showing. Those all white Jimmy Choo heels strapped around her legs and stopped at the lower part of her calf muscle. She had a matching all-white Jimmy Choo purse hanging from her side. I could even see her jewelry glistening as she got closer to my truck. Breaking my reverie Ahmir nodded at me swung the door open stepped out and played his position. Hello Ms. Lady look like you're riding shotgun tonight I'm gone hop in the back so the two of you can get acquainted. By the way I'm Ahmir your potential future brother-in-law.

Ahmir got into the back seat and I finally had Amari where I wanted her right by my side. We locked eyes embraced one another then peeled off into the night. After everyone introduced themselves, we decided Club 731 would be the spot for tonight. I'm gone purchase a booth in V.I.P section it comes with two bottles and five glow sticks that should kick the night off properly. The four of us agreed that would be the move so I pumped up the volume and let Gates preach for me. I ain' t trying to know your business, I ain' t trying to fall in love with you, see maybe he can love you different. I'm just trying to fuck with you and girl I'm trying to hit that pussy one time one time and be cool. What's up with it, what's up with you, what's up with you? Kevin Gates was blazing the woofers and Amari was moving to the beat cutting her eyes at me and everything. She didn't know it, but she was turning me on like a light switch I was ready to step into the spotlight so we can shine together. By the time we made it to Club 731 the parking lot was swarming with people. I parked in the paid parking area so that it would be more convenient for the ladies when the time come for is to make our exit. Any other time it wouldn't matter to me where I parked, but tonight was a special occasion plus I wanted the women to feel secured. It was two lines the regular line was wrapped around the club, and people were steady coming it wasn't even midnight yet. You could count on one hand how many people was in the V.I.P line so I knew this would be easy access. Upon making out entrance people were pointing and looking like we're super stars. Shanti and Amari was killing it you could see every definition of those women body. They kept it classy following close behind as we made out entrance. My guy Juice was at the door like always doing his thing. You know raising and cutting prices enforcing his charge fees if people wanted to enter or exit the club. As the club reached the capacity the more Juice would charge people to get in. I could respect his hustle because the man was calling numbers like the price is right. Juice gave Ahmir dap then we embraced each other had a few small words I paid him for the booth, and he pointed us in our direction. Making our way to the V.I.P section I could hear my guy D.J. Shaking it on the microphone in between him mixing.

Once we were seated in our booth a waitress quickly came over to assist us. Wearing nothing but a sleeveless top and booty shorts with Club 731 logos on them. The waitress was very polite as she took our order. Assuming she would get a good tip tonight or maybe it was the gorgeous women dipped in designer lace that intrigued her. Whatever it was shorty was giving some serious flirtatious signals as I placed an order for one color of each glow stick a bottle of 1800 Silver Tequila and a bottle of Grey Goose. Ahmir held out a fifty-dollar bill for the lady as she finished up and went to retrieve our order. "I don't know what it is, but shorty was mad thirsty." Ahmir stated before sparking a spliff. "Well the broad better go fix her a sprite because she doesn't have anything coming over here." Shanti said slapping hands with Amari then they went to snapping their necks and popping they gums like women do. I had to admit everybody was vibing like day ones. Ahmir passes me the medicated strain and I started getting lifted. Looking Amari in her eyes I just wanted her to feel comfortable not wanting to invade her space or nothing like that. I just laid back until the opportunity presented itself then I would go in for the kill. Timing is everything plus I know what the ladies so long as she was enjoying herself then that's all that mattered to me. Passing the aroma to Shanti I noticed the club was getting packed and we were making noise. Dudes was running up to the booth standing on couches trying their best to get some of what we were pumping in the atmosphere. Majority of the guys around town already knew who we were especially the d-boyz, the slab riders, even the local jokers. This was a normal night for Ahmir he was networking like Microsoft waving dudes off taking numbers even passing his number out. The club was three live and D.J. Shaking was blazing some hot tunes. I could see the waitress sparkle smoking from the back of the club as she made her way to our section. When she reached our booth, she had the glow sticks we ordered, a bucket of ice, and a complimentary bottle of Black Bel Aire Rose from the D.J. I guess D.J. Shaking it finally took a look at his phone and seen the text I sent him when I first walked in. She also informed us that she would bring the other two bottles out separately fifteen minutes apart. Why they do it like that I don't know, but if it's a show that they want then we were most definitely about to put one on for the city. Ahmir requested more cups for the crowd which was a good idea. I know good and well that I wasn't about to drink all that liquor I'm the designated driver I can't get wasted. Just as we popped the bottle of Rose and started pouring up and waving glow sticks. My guys D.J. Shaking It shouted Ahmir and I out over the club microphone and speakers. Not forgetting to mention the two beautiful women that accompanied us also. The four of us stood to our feet raised our cups and waned glow sticks to show respect for the homage he was showing us. Then he dropped the hottest tracks of the summertime. Dej Loaf ft. Big Sean back up off me they went retarded and turnt all the way up. I looked around at Shanti to see if the session was still burning, but it wasn't. I asked her did she put it out then she replied," Me, and my girl smoked that up then demanded for me to spark another one." I could tell that Shanti was on her level because she was getting aggressive. I grabbed Amari by the hand and looked in her eyes and noticed they were a little chinky we just smiled at one another I kissed her forehead and yelled tum up. I pour me another cup of the potion and put two spliffs in rotation. I came prepared I had five already rolled and a couple more grams left from what Ahmir gave me. Within another thirty minutes the waitress had brought two other bottles a bucket of ice and extra cups. Ahmir had two glow sticks behind his ears, a spliff hanging from his lips, and was passing out cups with shots of Grey Goose to whoever was in reach until the bottle was gone.

Chapter 4

It was almost two o'clock in the morning when I suggested that we blaze the picture book. We snapped up six photos two with all four of us, one with Ahmir and I. One with Shanti and Amari, one with Ahmir and Shanti, and one with Amari and I. When we left the picture booth Shanti and Ahmir made their way to the dance floor in the V.I.P. section. This was my chance to get more acquainted with Amari. I gripped her waistline and guided her back to the booth. It was still a fresh bottle of 1800 Silver Tequila on a bucket of ice. I pour us a couple of shots then sparked a spliff and we began to explore each other deepest intuition. She didn't know I was so open minded, and I didn't know she could be so understanding. I continued to compliment her style and grace Amari also reminded me of how much she admired the smell of my cologne. It was pushing three am and Ahmir and Shanti practically making love on the dance floor only with their clothes on. Amari and I agreed that Denny's would have the best breakfast food at this hour plus she invited me to spend the night with her. I was ready to run up out the club with her when I heard those words, but I couldn't spoil my sister and brother's moment. So, I just played it cool and enjoyed the rest of the spliff as Amari slow grinded on my lap. After about five or six songs of love making in the club that Shanti and Ahmir just pulled they came over and informed me that they were ready to roll. Without hesitating I slowly guided Amari off my crotch grabbed our pictures and the rest of the liquor then we made out exit. Exiting the club was like an autograph signing or red-carpet appearance. Ahmir and I was giving dap to guys, shaking hands, and showing respect as others embraced us. I even noticed Amari and Shanti fanning off an entourage of thirsty dudes, all the while keeping it sexy and classy. By the time we reached my truck it was a little after three am and the parking lot was jam packed with cars. Now was perfect for us to get off the radar before the club lets out. People gone get to spreading like wildfire and you know the police gone be patrolling like Mardi Gras. Bringing the Hemi to life after the four of us were seated comfortably Feeling a little tipsy, I checked to make sure everyone was alert and alive. "You're the one behind the wheel, Ceasar," the three of them said back. I kept my composure. "I am most definitely on my level, but I have it under control," I said. Adjusting all of my gadgets and turning on the headlights we were off in the wind. Maneuvering my way through traffic I took the nearest exit then merged onto Interstate forty. This would give me time to converse with Shanti and Ahmir to see what they wanted to do. If ya'll want to stop somewhere before I drop ya'll off I will because Amari and I have plans. "And what might that be?" asked Shanti leaning over the console smirking at Amari waiting for her to answer. Amari smiled and before she spoke, I cut in. For your information Shanti we are going to have breakfast then I will be spending my morning with Amari thank you. "Well ya'll have fun." Shanti stated before Ahmir cut her off. Check this bro it's a convenient store and Sonic next to our apartment. You can stop through there for me I will grab some for Shanti and me then we're good. You and Amari can go tum up the after party. Laughter erupted and Shanti leaned up giving Amari that look and nodding in approval. I did as instructed and stopped by the store and Sonic for Ahmir. 3:42 a.m. the clock read by the time I dropped Ahmir and Shanti off at our apartment. I finally had Amari's attention, and I was not about to abuse it. The R&B slow jams were penetrating the subwoofers at the appropriate volume. Noticing that Amari was wide awake singing and working her body to the music. She didn't know it, but she was turning me on some serious, by being herself which earned her an A plus in my book. Showing consideration, I turned down the volume and suggested that we get our food to go. I didn't want to be out any later than we had to. She agreed that would be fine with her and just like that Amari and I were on our way to better days.

•.. €...

"Hey, baby do you want the rest of your French fries.", Shanti yelled from the kitchen table to Ahmir who was in his bedroom closet fumbling with the vacuumed sealed packages he had inside a duffel bag. "Naw, ma I good!" Ahmir yelled back to his fiancé with his deep voice echoing through the apartment. "Oh, baby I feel so good." Shanti said as she was undressing in front of Ahmir while he was twisting a spliff. I really enjoyed myself and Amari was very nice I actually like her she's not ratchet like a lot of the other women I meet. We exchanged for future references plus we have a lot in common. "I bet the two of you did." stated Ahmir nonchalantly. You probably know the woman whole life story knowing you sweetheart. It's all good continue to use your counseling tactics on people. It will pay off one day you know practice make perfect ma. "Yeah whatever." stated Shanti with a sassy attitude. Keep on joking Ahmir, but when I finish school and get my master's degree, I'm going into business for myself then I will be making one hundred dollars an hour for my counseling tactics. Then we will see who has jokes when I'm laughing to the bank cashing them checks. "That's exactly right sweetheart." stated Ahmir in a low tone. You know I love you like non other and I'm your biggest supporter when it comes to anything you chose to do. Now get that naked booty in between them sheets it's four in the morning and its Mr. Nasty time. Without saying a work Shanti was butt naked in between the sheets purring for daddy to join her. Attempting to set the mood I turned off all the lights then adjusted the stereo to some soothing slow jams. Sitting at head of the bed I sparked a spliff then took a few pulls from the Cali strain before putting it out. Just a habit I had developed over the years. Shanti was rubbing and caressing my shaft and pulling my body towards her. I rolled over onto my back then Shanti guided my boxer briefs from around my waist. She gently massaged my rock-hard massive chocolate cock with her palms. Shanti was sucking and slurping my juicy cock while tickling and caressing my balls wither her freshly done pedicure at the same time.

Sending my body into a sensational overload she continued to take charge. Straddling on top of me then sliding my shaft between her honey pot until I penetrated her juicy nectar. Shanti let out soft moans and light screams as she grinded and bounced her firm booty up and down my chocolate pole. Kissing and licking from her beautiful face to her luscious breast and I smacked that ass in approval every time she came down allowing me to dig deeper and deeper. Allowing her to have her way with me Shanti made sweet love to daddy dick, and then I was fast asleep. The next morning, I was alerted by my cell phone ringing off the hook. It wasn't even eleven o' clock yet and I had fifteen missed calls. Knowing that I needed to get up and take care of my clientele anyway. Strolling through my phone I already knew who it was and what they wanted. I sent a quick text informing them to come through the spot and it was understood. It was almost 2:00 p.m. when Shanti came crawling out the bedroom. She was still naked looking sexy as ever waking from her slumber. I'm glad you're awake sweetheart because I done worked up and appetite. Do you mind going to Taco Bell or somewhere and get us something to eat? Shanti agreed well can I at least freshen up and put some clothes on first daddy. Of course, take you rime am I know you had an extravaganza last night not to mention that you were an animal this morning. Laughing out loud Shanti did as her future husband requested. When Shanti returned with the groceries, we sat at the kitchen table and enjoyed our lunch together. Finishing up a triple decker cheeseburger and a loaded baked potato that Shanti brought back from Wendy's for me. I guzzled down the orange Hi-C drink and looked Shanti in her wonderful eyes then spoke.

Baby you know what I like and how I like it and that's one reason I love you unconditionally ma you're my everything. Sometimes I wonder what I would do without you or how far I will go with you. "Well daddy you know the sky is the limit. I'm your motivation, your friend, and lover. I will be whatever you need me to be I'm here for you daddy." Shanti stated with sincerity in her voice. Okay now that my battery is recharged, I think it's time for an evening session.

Since you had all the fun last night and took advantage of me. It's m y turn to get some exercise in sweetheart plus we have a long day. Ceasar hasn't called or texted so I know he's occupied with his date. Shanti got wet from the thought of what Ahmir wanted to do with her. "I want you too daddy, come love all over me I don't mind just be nice and don't hurt me.", Shanti stated in a seductive tone with lust in her eyes. Before I realized it three and a half hours passes by Shanti and I had been making sweet love all day. I forgot my phone was on the kitchen table. When we got up to shower it was 6:45 p.m. and I couldn't get enough of Shanti's long legs and jiggly booty. We made love in the shower standing up you know I got superman stamina I'm no amateur. After the hut shower session, I put on my swim trunks and a pair of 2013 Airmax tennis shoes. When I got to my phone there were all kinds of weird text messages from my ex girlfriend. If I wasn't mistaken, I could have made a bet that his chick was somewhere close by stalking me. Ignoring the delirious messages, I called my partner back and told him that it was all good for him to come get that. I had two packages left and my guy was on his way to get one of em. Shanti was in the bedroom getting dressed when I heard someone beating at the door.

Irritated from the unannounced beating I didn't think to ask who it was. I just swung the door open with aggression and to my surprise it was the police. The officer claimed that it was a disturbance call and shots fired from this complex. Plus, the lady in the parking lot says that her boyfriend Mr. Ahmir stole her car keys and she wanted them back or she is going to press charges. Just as I was getting ready to step outside to see who the lady was making these accusations, another officer stepped through the door and the first words from his mouth were that he could smell marijuana coming from inside the apartment. With no trust for the cops and not wanting to go to jail the first thought that came to my head was run. That's exactly what I did played it off with the officer as if I was trying to explain myself. Right when the opportunity presented itself, I pushed the officer to the side with a juke move then struck out running like Emmitt Smith.

To Be Continued...

Up next is the revealing of the poetry by Philosopher himself. The art is manifested from within we all have it, but how we choose to express it is key. It's time to step up and be that example for all eyes to see. If you dream it you can achieve it, if you pursue it you can do it. If I can inspire one individual to live a path that's built from righteousness then my mission here is complete.

Stability

Living in my mind I never felt so great and comfortable.
Maybe because I'm forced to make peace while I live
the heart of the jungle. Memories of intimate acts
shared with many varieties of beautiful women.
Some are my favorite to this very moment.
I could still bore the energy and ecstasy from encounters years ago!
Who will understand me?
If l confessed, I'm caught in a love
Web of multiple women, with only so many words left unspoken.
I find myself grieving with many mixed emotions.

Undesirable Love

Take heed from the art of seduction although beauty
is fleeting while charming is deceptive.
Persuasion from the opposite sex appealing
intractable for the emotional plane.
Holding back with resistance trying to stay committed
to the commitment All the while temptation
Reveals to be
Oh, so tempting. Falling victim to the powers possessed
by the possessor Eagar to keep composure
Feeling weak
At the knees as intimacy makes its closure. Sparks
fly let the electricity Flow through the body
Like a
Mysterious current through traffic. Euphoria at its
finest a complete Feeling of satisfaction.

Inevitable Love

Loyalty is far and in between now days. In search of
something worth holding On to in so many ways.
The natural healing that comes from the feeling of being loved
Once I dreamed of the inevitable Love connection.
Flying into my world like the symbolic Turtle dove.
What was once, but a daydream is
Now loving me consistently. In reality, I know this
is a blessing the unexpected happened
To me.
There is no time for second guessing!
Stranger Than Most
Now tell me love
Can't be dangerous. The person
I been sharing my bed with is a complete stranger.
Funny how I thought
That I knew you. Very sad how
You deceived me because I was the one down from you.
Got me striving for Perfection because it's never late
For correction. I'm just shaking my head because I saw this coming and
I read between the lines. Sad to say
Love had me blind, but curious. I know its's someone who loves the way
That I do and feels the things that I feel.
In search of my soulmate, someone who makes
me feel like every day is my birthday.

Love Note

In search of a
Peace of mind. Is there a reason
Why this love I feel is one of a kind. I have been
Deceived before, but
Im sure not this time. Its
Truly amazing the way I draw strength from deep
Within, but surely
It's a blessing how my lover
Can be my best friend. A place I can call home
The sound of her
Voice is like a love song. How
Could this feeling grow deeper? Could I
Be tempted by her
Genuine ways and gorgeous features?
Similar to a fantasy come true I honestly feel God's skill
Power manifesting
Through you I don't believe in
False courage my guidance and understanding makes me pray
For a beautiful marriage.

Stranger Than Most

Now tell me love
Can be dangerous. The person
I been sharing my bed with is a stranger.
Funny how I thought
Then I knew you. Very said how
You deceived me because I was the one down for you.
Got me striving for
Perfection because its never too late
For correction. Im just shaking me head because I
Seen this coming and
I read between the lines. Sad to say
Love had me blind, but cautious. I know its someone
Who loves the way
That I do and feel the things that I feel.
In search of my soul mate someone who makes me feel
Like every day is my
Birthday. I need real loved filled
With kisses and hugs plus a genuine touch. Now that's
Passionate and sacred.
I need it on a daily basis come
Give me my motivation. Allow me to salute you dreams
And visons of us
Sharing our intuitions. Not only is
This real love, but baby this is big business.
Let us grow and build together
Let's make this last forever.

Actions

Every dog has its day and every soul eventually finds his way.
Thru the rain and the storm, we seek a solid
foundation that we can form.
Just as April showers bring May flowers. Let
everything we do be for a purpose every
Minute and hour.
From the seeding stage cleanup to harvest
season. For Every Cause is an effect.
So, let our actions speak for good enough reason.
We can't change principle but we
Can master the ability to actually see thru what's visible.
With knowledge comes Understanding.
Foolishness will not be tolerated, but greatness gets demanded.
We must learn from our Mistakes.
Let's not wait on tomorrow from what we can accomplish today.
For hard work bring great Rewards.
Let's enjoy the fruits of our labor and live our life with happiness and joy.

Temptation

How many words can explain what I'm feeling,
and How many languages do I have to
Speak to convince you that I'm willing?
Even when you're not around I can feel your sexual Healing. Chills
running down my spine and fantasies living in my mind.
I'm traveling through a tunnel of love memorized
by the scent and glares from the candlelight
Which twinkle like the stars above.
My lovely queen awaits me in a rose pedal filled Hot tub.
Caught in a trance wishing I could freeze this Moment and it would
Never end.
I may speak in parables so please don't let me confuse
you. God's most sacred gift to mankind
Wonder why I salute you.
Drift away with me and you may witness my deepest ambition.
Don't speak just listen as my heart beats a Passionate tune that's owe so
Ever full filling.

Anonymous

Infatuated from the touch of the Price possessor.
Who has the capabilities to stimulate?
The most insatiable
A way with words that are precisely Chosen.
With tactics and strategies that are immaculate and phenomenon.
Penetrating so sharply you would have mistaking It for a heart that
Was broken.
If you were asleep you can best believe that now he has awoken.
Surprised some say astounded from the works of one who was cut
Well rounded.
The finishing touches to a masterpiece demanding
an encore with applauses and shouts
For a breath taking Series!

I Found You

You're the one I want in my life. It's not A secret we been creeping and
Having private meetings.
Then we question it like what's the reason, but
believe me I think about you daily.
I want you to have
My baby, but I got patience. I know we can
make it. I fell victim to a love
Crime my heart was
Taken. So many years I couldn't see the signs.
I was trying to replace it. Unfortunately I was mistaken.
Searching to find that certain somebody to
plead my case with. I have to look
Her in the eyes and testify.
Baby you one in a million, you the best and I',
Here to remind you. The reverie of
You having my children.
I love it when I'm stroking and working inside
you. Who reliable to expound
How we do?
Only me! Loving you unconditionally, loving
you until the end of time. Baby come
Share your emotions with me.

Love Note #2

You stole my heart
From the very beginning. Now I
Can't live without you. As if you were my
prescription, my medicine, my insulin.
You can call me and addict because
My body feigns for you. I'm addicted and I'm not ashamed.
Head over hills for my Sweetheart. Let's takes a trip without
Looking back. I'm connected with you like
a door to its Latch. The love we
Share has a purpose. With so many
Words I can paint a picture about what I'm feeling.
All the while caught
In this concept. Deep down I wanna
Expound so the world may know. We're living substantial!
From the out skirts Looking in one may think this
Is pretend. Loving you until my last breath.
I have found my
Peace of mind. Loving you is no longer blind.

Paradise

"As the sun rises." Shining like a beautiful creation
and sign of new life. The Rocky
Mountain sides which
Are visible from so far away, yet and still seem so close.
The motionless waves of the Ocean. Symbolizing
Beauty like he sunset. With attractions of
artwork and relaxation, as if it was
Magic. The roaring
Tidal waves that thunder like the clouds of the sky.
The deep blue waters concealing the world's most
Mysterious and unknown secrets. A kingdom of
in surety And security were you can
Let loose and be free.
The reverie of palm trees and ocean shores.
That pineapple sweet life, stretched
Hummers and chauffeurs.
Followed with love making in the finest sheets of
them Hotel suite floors. "Do you dream
Of paradise?"

Love Connection

The love connection
That we share is not perfect, but
It's truly a blessing. Admiring everything about you.
When it comes to
Loving me, I know it's no limits to
What you will do. Your actions speak louder than Words. Plus, your
Loyalty is true and pure as proverbs.
I know that your soulmate. I acknowledge what we have and I
Refuse to let you slip away. I'm
Willing to please and provide for your each
and every Need by any means
Necessary. Thinking ahead while planning
carefully. My prayers were answered so
Have no worries
Our journey is not complete.
Know that we are one step closer to our destiny.

Listening

I can hear you
Heart and it's calling out my name.
I can read your body language and it's doing the same.
If I miss out
On your blessing baby then I'm the
One to blame. You're the true definition of a
platinum award Winner. You're going
To love this treatment from my love
Session. Followed with a candlelit dinner. Rose
pedals in your Bathtub. Aroma
Therapy to set the mood. How you
Want it? "Fast or slow!" I know you like it
deep and Rough. It's guaranteed
To go down tonight like the world
Trade center. Sweetheart you official like a referee whistle.
I'm promising you Quality your presence is enough
For me. I love you unconditionally.

To Be Loved

Just how many ways can I please you is A question I ask myself. So
Many thoughts of
Living life and loving one another until my death.
Oh what a feeling to be Loved by someone
Who appreciates your presence? I'm pretty sure
we All have been taken for granted.
How considerate of
An individual who understands a mutual connection.
One that's beneficial and protected.
I seek refuge away
From anything that's negative. I know the
feeling of being betrayed or neglected.
I don't fear being
Corrected. Listening and observing carefully so I
won't Miss out on my blessing. Rather
They pour rain showers
On me, or I have to go get it. To be loved by
thousands possibly millions. Oh, what a
Feeling to be loved.
I'm soaking it all in until I'm finished.

Expression

It's not a day passing me by. That this woman's loyalty doesn't cross my
Mind.
Understanding, outgoing is the words to describe her character.
Divine, hardworking she's
A natural born leader. With vision and demeanor.
Cherishing her Gifts knowing, she
The package. We rock together the two of us are like a bad habit.
It's hard to break its impossible
To fold. My queen compliments her king. She
comes first, but we journey together as
One with
Not one story going untold. Proceed with caution
be mindful don't Let the expression
Mislead you.
If l stated my mission was complete. I only live
to enjoy what we do. Who knows what
Tomorrow
Will bring forth? Name thee who has experienced true love.
One may lead you astray
But, one may crown a soulmate. We demonstrate from our actions.
Knowing love can be Blind or
A fatal attraction

Session

I'm the love doctor
Class is in session. In the streets
I'm such a gentleman, but in the sheets I'm so aggressive.
We can battle for
Your love pushes and shoves like
Tug a war. Welcome to my classroom where all activities are orchestrated
From my rules. Be cautious because
Your body is on the menu. You are the main
ingredient to my secret recipe.
I got this spice for your life
I promise to play nice. I'm packing what they are slacking.
Only when I
React is to your every reaction.
Call me the love machine. I go commando like the marines.
Rather on top or underneath. I stand up in between
You like the Statue of Liberty. At ease while you
journey with me enjoy the breeze.

Passion

Hold your tone just listen. I have you weak at
the Knees. Only from a smile and
Intuition. Be cautious
Of the submission. No, I'm not the one to judge
you I'm the one who loves you. Like
Non-other. Will you help?
Keep me out of trouble. I just love to hustle, but
that's any form of fashion. A man of my
Caliber gotta have it.
I'm aware of what you have poking out from behind.
With all due respect I won't grab it unless you ask me.
I draw motivation from your loving. Your kiss and hugs.
If whatsoever you happen to feel that.
You are more into stimulation that penetration.
Know That I can co-adjust to
The situation.
Your passionate ways and affectionate taste
are Very persuasive. Your emotions
Mean more to me
So, I show gratitude. It's in my nature only to
respect it. Now this something worth
Holding on to.

Mindful

We share that type of love that grows deeper and
deeper every day. Just from the feeling
I get when your
Away. Keeps me looking forward to the next
time I See your face. With so much
To relate to within out relation.
If something calls for your absence and I'm not in your presence. I
Could still feel
Your essence and energy. Causing my heart to
beat with anticipation. This woman
Is my motivation.
I need her on a daily basis. "Why not?" fulfill
me with your sexual healing!
Don't feel alarmed
If I find you appealing. Let me inform you that
you satisfy my every feeling. For
Any acts that
We may commit, sweetheart I'm always willing.
You are gifted point-blank period.
Your bio belongs
In a series. I'm blessed just to share the experience
that we're living. The modern day
Goddess sheading light for

The ones that's watching. How wise of myself to
clarify all of your greatness that you
Possess. It's evident
To see the path, you lead is built from righteousness.

Vibrations

Can you picture what?
I'm seeing? Do you hear what I'm hearing?
That's the sound of emotions please have no fear.
Just listen pay close Attention as it whispers in your ear.
You feel it's taking over your body. Baby that's
the reason I'm here. To set you
Free now spread your wings and
Live your life to the fullest. Know that I'm
here for your Comfort. Come sport
Me like a new hoody. So, I can
Protect you from the storm and keep your body warm.
Caressing and holding
You through the night. The feeling appealing so
right we're loving under the moonlight.
As the sunrise we
Gazing into each other eyes. Sweetheart
No lie you are the love of my life. Feeling complete and free. Sometimes
I feel weak getting lost in our memories.

Rain Drops

With the rain dripping down my window
Pane. My heart's beating a melody that's one in the same.
Who should I
Turn to? Who can I trust?
While praying for deliverance yet, still my heart lust.
Trying to control
My body's temptation. Risen above
The influence, but show no signs of weakness Knowing that
what they have to offer will only
Hinder me. Acknowledge my faults correct where I was mistaken.
Master my abilities to perfect
My will. Controlling what I was once controlled with.
Know that I'm Destined to achieve what's
In store for me. Proceed with caution but have no fear.
Even as the rain
Pours. The sky still projects crystal clear.

Confessions

We believe in love Making. Feeling secure with the
Look in your eyes baby. You so sincere the thought of losing you
Puts fear in my heart, knowing you
Are my soulmate. Refusing to let anyone tear us apart.
Exposing my Confessions. I'm addicted
To your love and I know you're my blessing. You free my mind from
Confusion and frustrations. At times
It seems like a fantasy or reverie, but in reality we complete one
Another. Now that makes us
A team. I love tossing and turning with you through the night. Waking
Up to you feel oh so right. Why
Not pick up where we left off. Must I remind you that your one of
A kind. The proper preparations
Have been made, I'm ready to love you until the end of time.

Do You Mind

Do you mind? If I was to whisper a couple of
riddles in your ear. Spilling the potent
Potion in yo section.
May cause you to shake and shiver, don't be afraid.
My verses are much needed Like clinic aid.
I can be sweet like lemonade, but I cut and
slice so sharply like a switch blade.
Do you mind?
If I was to inform you of your worth. Please pay
close Attention and listen. Correct me
If I go wrong or
If it's anything I forget to mention. Do you
mind? If I was to get up on your level.
Unfolding and revealing
Your deepest secrets within minutes. Your
demeanor says it all. Do you Mind? If
I stay consistent
With my persistence through summertime, winter, spring, or fall.

Fifth period

Mesmerized by her wonderful eyes. I find myself, caught in
A trance.
Once again in my mind a party is taking place as Fifth period begins.
She walks
In and takes her seat as classy as the day before.
Trying not to stare at
Her beautiful features. All thanks to God for this gorgeous creature.
Enjoying
The scent from her fancy perfume, which
polluted the air when she entered
The classroom
She doesn't know it, but I admire her every attribute.
Contemplating on a reason Why the two
Of us should be speaking. Keeping my composure
only wishing that fifth period didn't have
To be over.
Interrupting my reverie, the lunch bell rang
crushing my fantasy with whom
I admire.
Wanting her in my arms I felt satisfied making my way

To the lunchroom only if
One knew the connection from the energy in my fifth period classroom.

I Need

My heart cries
Out for righteousness. The essence
Of my woman's love fulfills my soul with happiness.
While dwelling amongst Strangers and misguided creatures.
My guidance from the most high gives me a peace of mind.
Praying for an abundance of prosperity within
My life. Taking full responsibility for every
opportunity and opening door
That awaits me. I need my
Woman's sexual healing. The feeling from
her touch, the Warmth from her
Body, the taste from her kisses the
Scent from her fragrance. I need my woman's love on the daily basis.
I know it's sincere, I need to be near and one with you.

Acknowledge

How many take for granted what we do have?
Who actually gives credit where credit
Is due? Very
Foolish when you let something good slip right
from under you. Acknowledging your hard
Work and admiring
Where you are in life. A strong black woman
that you truly are. I'm really impressed
The way you
Maintain under all the stress. Blessed and
possess Powers that are astounding.
Showing leadership
With your influential ways. What a great influence
you Have on our young woman
Today. Someone
Should worship the ground you walk on. A self-
made Queen in her own comfort
Zone. What
Credibility you show, one who inspires and encourages.
I acknowledge all that you do because you are a Great Samaritan.

True Love

Love can be blind
Or misguided leading to pain
And sorrow. True love comes from within.
It's the essence of a moment that
Captures hearts and fulfill
Cold dark empty spaces. True love is divine
and pure the Force is very strong.
The energy so powerful that
It builds up motivation and gives strength to persist in adversity.
Be cautious about
Who you share you love with.
Acknowledge when you are truly being loved.
True love comes with patience,
Discipline, and wisdom.
One must be willing to sacrifice at the spare of any moment.
True love will
Heal broken spirits and come
In different forms of fashion. To truly be
loved is a gift from the most high.
One may have to search
For that love then again that love may be at your fingertips.
You have to see
The signs and read between
The lines. Knowing love manifest itself and just my wear a disguise.

My Woman

My woman is like the finest gold and purest silver.
All the richest in the world wouldn't
Amount to her loving. Which overflows like the Nile River.
My woman stands for Capitalism
Commanding Queen of the castle. She is the captain of my Elite.
I refuse to hold back on loving her.
I will not retreat when it comes to protecting
her. My woman is the antidote for
World
Peace. She is the silent whisper that calms
the lions and Wolves of the wild.
My woman
Is tender, she is any and everything you can
ask for in her gender. She deserves
To be head
Of this nations, most importantly she is my woman.

Evident

Look into my eyes express what it is you see,
I'm the True definition of a man with
Quality. For
The ones who may want a taste it's gone cost a small fee.
I'm finger licking good well down To the last
Drop. Call me candy man you scream my name non-stop.
Come bless me with your Presence
Your greetings is my pleasure, I know my love is
needed in Times of desperate measures.
I can be
Addictive let that be a warning. My sex drive is very high
Every night and every
Morning.
I know what you like if you try me on for
size I can't Promise that I won't
Bite. Fast
Forward from your past because I'm nothing like you last.
I'm one in a million, now
If you feel
It's too much then I can adjust like the chameleon.

Imagine

Do you imagine the two of us laying up?
Inside of the mansion? I'm going hard baby like
I'm trying to win The Heisman. Do
You imagine me keeping
Your body pleased satisfaction? I'm open minded
to your thoughts. Girl I'm your
Best friend. Do you
Imagine? Living life in paradise not worried about prices, shopping
In designer Stores popping tags
Without a budget you gotta love it. Do you
imagine? Me kissing you from your
Anus to where your back
Bend clean up around your necklace. I do
this to perfection Girl I'm a sex
King. Do you imagine?
Pulling up in foreign cars? European across
the dashboard everything digital
Making love while we record press rewind then fast forward.

Sensation

I just want to get lost in your love, and let it take me away.
Can we drift like the ocean shores and?
The tidal waves?
I know you deep and wet no disrespect I'm just speaking the truth.
Please do not disturb or interrupt just follow my rules
Your body language got me caught in a trance it's like a brand new
Bentley coupe or Mercedes Benz. Now when you're riding by
My side it's no regrets it's do or die.
I just want to live
My life, loving you is one of a kind.
I don't have to
Think twice baby come and be my wife.
Loving you until
The end of time let me continue to blow your mind.

Short Story 3

No relation regarding anyone outside this
context is intended by the author.

Chapter 1

Knowing that the out of shape officers weren't seeing a picture of me while in foot pursuit. I know the neighborhood all too well to let them jam me up like that. My white boy Red and his fiancé live behind my apartment complex. Which is a neighborhood of houses that lead back into the city limits. Red live on South St. In a tan house. Which was perfect because a six-foot wooden fence separated a dark alley from his street. I was running so fast and hand that I gained good yardage on the officers from the take off. By the time I made it through the alley and jumped the fence the officers were officially smoked. They were out of my sight all I could see were their flashlights reflecting through the darkness. Applying what strength that remained in my body and legs to make it to Red's house. Just to my advantage when I reached his driveway pushing myself to the distance. He and his fiancé were running out the door fumbling their car keys trying to get to me. The moment I saw them coming out of their door. Everything in me gave out and I collapsed right in the driveway. With nothing left in me I crawled towards the front door as Red and his fiancé assisted me. Once inside the house I laid on the living room floor out of breath and out of my mind. Red began informing me that he was listening to the police scanner. So, when the disturbance call to the address came through, he assumed it was me. He exclaimed that he didn't pay it no mind. Knowing I'm not the one to be involved with any shenanigans. Now, when word came over the scanner that some lady was claiming that her boyfriend stole her keys to a Camaro. He knew it was me that's when he tuned into the channel. Five minutes later there was a foot pursuit. Black male blue shorts approximately five foot nine inches running south bound. That's when he and his fiancé came running, but by that time they made it out the door I was in the driveway. My adrenaline was pumping rapidly and I was too hot trying to catch my breath. I had been smoking Kush and sipping tussin ex doctor prescribed all day long. Out of nowhere all hell broke loose and I started puking up my insides uncontrollably. I mean everything I just ate and then some. It hurt so bad I was out of commission, but it continued to come out of me. As I erupted in the middle of the living room floor Red told me it was ok. He had me and to let it on out. Then he instructed his fiancé to get the garbage can from the kitchen, towels from the bathroom, and some of his changing clothes from the bedroom. Once I was finished, I gained a little composure. Then I changed to the plaid shorts and white beater Red's fiancé got for me. Feeling concerned if someone saw me or not Red was quick on his feet. So, as I was changing, he asked me if there was any where he could take me. Wanting to get me completely off this side of town was a good idea. I was so distraught and in pain that I couldn't speak I just shook my head yes. Red cleaned me up and I managed to walk to his vehicle then signaled him towards my destination. Lexy was this young chick twenty-two years old that I met a month or two ago. She had been trying to get in my boxers, but out of respect of what I already had going on I never took it there. I didn't wat to add her to the equation knowing she wasn't prepared for what I had to offer. I kept it mutual with her when she came to shop with me sometimes, we would smoke and ride around the city together. She even cooked for me a few times so in my eyes she was just a friend. Lexy demanded more, now two or three weeks prior to what jus took place. She called me for some Kush as usual it was just another day another dollar for me. I just so happened to be alone doing numbers like a trap star, so I instructed her to come on through the spot. When Lexy showed up she had intentions on getting what she really wanted. She wore nothing but a flowered dress that stopped a few inches above her kneecaps. It connected around her neck but her shoulders and back were revealing. Lexy was dark brown skin complexion she stood five foot three inches maybe one hundred and twenty-five pounds very petite nice round B cups and a firm backside. She was average but she had a good reputation. Her own car and house, no kids you know things of that nature. When she arrived, I let her in then went and sat back down at my coffee table in the living room. I was fixing up the sack she ordered but when I looked back up, she had me cornered. The words that she spoke next were you gone quit running from me. She was standing front and center in a tight little dress with her hands on her hips, and all I could do was smile. She was correct I couldn't run anymore so I reached under her dress and got aroused immediately. She wore no panties or bra and her vagina was juicy and soft. Plus, she had it shaved smooth just how I like it. I couldn't help myself so I raided up her dress to witness her possessions. To my surprise it was very attractive she actually turned me on. I guided her to the bedroom and blessed her with something she had never experienced before. Some grade A quality penis stroke for stroke. Ever since then we been going steady it was all copasetic. Vicky is Lexy mother she also did business with me. Vicky would give me some flirtatious vibes when she came to shop with me. I just disregarded it one I had enough going on two she most definitely wasn't my type. Vicky lived with Lexy on the eastside of town. I knew I was welcome there at any time. That's where I got Red to take me, but when I got their Lexy wasn't home just Vicky. Of course, she let me in with a worried look on her face. Red explained to her what happened while I went to Lexy room and passed out in her bed. Moments later Vicky came in and put warm towels on my neck and back. Then later that night I felt Lexy kissing and talking to me. I was in so much pain I didn't gain composure until 3:00 a.m. in the morning. Once I gained composure, I realized that I lost my phone while running from the cops. My biggest concern was Shanti I know she's a true soldier, but still it didn't sit right with me knowing I put her in harm's way. With no way of contacting her all I could do was sit back and wait. For word to come through about what transpired after I took off. My thought process raced 1,000 miles per hour of the worst-case scenarios. What if they try to charge her with the narcotics that's in my crib? Even though the 45 cal. Kimber with the lemon squeeze was clean and in my brother's name. There's no justification when you have controlled substances with intent to resale around any type of firearm. Not to mention I'm already a two-time convicted felon. The game I been playing just ended drastically. I needed to get in touch with Ceasar a.s.a.p. All the events that took placed within the last 48 hours replayed over and over again. I tried to figure out what went wrong then it hit me. Essence she was standing right there with the law when I took off running. Disturbing the peace about my vehicle that was in her name. She was even in the 2012 Ford Fusion I purchased for her also. I couldn't believe she had the audacity to clown me like that with the police. I have to admit I didn't cut all ties with Essence we were still creeping and having private meetings. Plus, I still had a key to the apartment we once shared, so I was in and out here and there. I was food to Essence we had our ups and downs, but still I had two new cars in her name building up her credit. She had access to unlimited amounts of Kush at any time she wanted it. Essence was something like my first I showed her a lot and taught her about life and herself in general. It was vice versa when I got with her, I matured my thinking and elevated my game. This was years ago before Shanti was even in the equation. Essence had a funky attitude she stood five feet to inches one hundred and fifty-three pounds. Cute face small waist chocolate skin complexion pigeon-toed thick tin the thigh and hips real model material. She had a decent personality, but that attitude was toxic as you can see, she can be poison. I never thought she would play it like this. Where did she come from last, I knew she was working around the hours this took place? Deep down I knew I would have to face her again and converse about what she just caused. Mean whole I was restless and in so much pain my stomach was in knots I could barely walk and I didn't have my phone. My phone was like my life line I ate off that phone not to mention all the mouths I was feeding off that phone. This was a time I needed to be networking, but I didn't know a lot of numbers by hand they were programmed in my phone. I had plans people owed me money and everything most importantly I didn't know if Shanti was safe or not.

Chapter 2

Soon as day broke I was up and ready to find a resolution. All I had on me was my wallet that contained a little over $500.00 inside it. My first step was to buy a phone. I managed to take a quick shower in Lexy bathroom, but I had to put the clothes Red gave me back on. After showering I laid back in bed next to Lexy enduing the pain, but the shower didn't help ease it. Lexy was my friend more than anything so I blessed her and gave her what she wanted. It's a good chance she wouldn't come across another man like me. I had respect for her so I kept the proper distance between us. I had a lot going on and she had some knowledge of it so she respected that and played her position. Not in a million years would I have ever thought that I would be dependent of her any in form of fashion. I felt awkward lying next to her for some reason like I was out of place or something. I didn't know what to do so I waited for her to wake up before making any moves. She woke up about 7:00 or 7:30 a.m. that morning which was still early. I began to fill her in on the game plan and what took place the night before not leaving out one detail. Like I said Lexy was my friend she knew I had a lady or two. There was no reason for me to lie to her. She respected I she was finally happy to have me where she wanted in her domain. Word travel so fast that when I was informing her on what happened and some information that I needed her to get. She was already on point one of her friends knew Shanti's cousin. Come to find out the police let Shanti go. She was at her cousin house waiting around for me. A little weight was lifted from my shoulders knowing Shanti was secured. Now, all I needed was her car keys for a few hours. Of course, she agreed, but she wasn't about to let me out her sight without getting what she wanted. So, I treated her to an early morning sample. Just enough to get me by for the moment. After my encounter with Lexy I washed myself off then pulled into traffic.

Nervous as a crack head in a drug store because now I was on the run. I knew the cops were looking for me possibly my brother also. I kept my cool and handled my business like a man. With the loss I just took it was time to collect from the ones that owed me. Merging into traffic like nothing happened my first stop was the Dollar General. While there I purchased a $50.00 prepaid phone programmed it then called Shanti immediately. The sound of her voice brought joy to my soul. No one could love me like this woman; she was the chosen one. We talked for almost an hour she told me all the details that took place after I ran. She informed me about what the cops were asking her while they searched my crib. Then she mentioned what they found and all that. I told her long as she was safe nothing else mattered it could be replaced in due time. Instructing her about the few moves I had to make and that I needed her to sit tight for a couple hours. Then she could come get me and we could go to my mom's crib for a while. Shanti was cool with that. Then she threw me for a loop when she stated. That there were a few things we needed to discuss. My mind began to wonder just what that could be. Shanti, the cool, calm, collected type. She can be hard to read sat times. Who knows I just had to wait and see? Meanwhile, I had to go by my guy L spot and scoop up that bread he owed me. When I called Ceasar he was already on point. He also mentioned that he seen the whole situation go down. Essence was outside the spot with the police. When he was on his way to pick up some changing clothes. Instead of pulling into our complex he pulled into the next one down and watched. He said he was blowing my phone up, but kept getting my voicemail. Then two or three minutes later he saw me jetting pass the police. He knew then it was some foolishness in the game. Ceasar then stated. That he would call me later on his break because he was on the floor. Working his machine operator job. I informed him that the cops probably got my phone and this would be my new number. We both screamed love then ended the call. I pulled up at L spot without notice. Already knowing what he was on trapping and controlling traffic. Five minutes after waiting outside his house in the driveway. He walked up from behind and hopped in the blazer with me. "What's up Ahmir I thought you were a sale." L stated with excitement in his voice. He immediately put a flame to a dutch then passed it back and forth getting faded. During the smoke session, I filled L in on what had taken place the night before. I could tell from the expression on his face that he was disappointed with the news. He knew with me out the picture things would get tight for him. Not wanting to rain on his parade. I informed him that everything was going to be ok. I still got the plug and I got stacks so we gone make it shake this weekend. All I'm doing now is collecting from the ones that owe me and laying low. Plus, all my guys on deck so it's a green light for him whenever he ready." Well, I got that together for you. I have to run in the house and snatch it up really quick. Then you can get off the radar and get somewhere safe, as you can see, I'm making noise around here.", Stated L before he hopped out the truck to get the cash. See that's why I deal with L he's worthy and he keep something going. His phone was rattling like a freak nik hotline. Cars were pulling up like a drive-thru, you would have thought he was selling hot cakes. This fool had more traffic than I did and I was supplying him. I thought to myself aw yeah, it's time to roll. I didn't want to see to many people things were hot for me right now. I can't afford for these clowns to dial 528-CASH on me trying to get a hot tip. When L came back out, I counted the cash. It was on point $2,500 then I purchased a qtr. oz of Kush from him for my troubles. We dapped it up and I gave him my new number and peeled out. L was one of the few people I would let owe me small chunks of cash. Everybody else only owed me for small stuff like qtr. Pounds an ounces. I spent the next two hours pulling down on cats collecting whatever I could. When I made it back to Lexy I accumulated almost $4,000? Don't get me wrong I wasn't rich, but I sure wasn't asking nobody for anything. That's what I'm grinding for trying to stack six or seven figures. It's was $2,500 sashed at the apartment there's a good chance the cops overlooked it. Forced t wit and go check on that at least until Ceasar got off work. There were valuables in my apartment that's worth money also. Shanti mentioned that the police were taking things out my spot. Upon entering Lexy's house, I smelled food in the air. Which was perfect because I was paranoid to stop anywhere for food. Jackson, TN, a small city and word travel fast. I couldn't afford to bump into anyone that I didn't have to. As I rested on the sofa Ms. Vicky walked in the living room with a plate for me. Eggs, toast, and turkey sausage, you sure were reading my mind Ms. Vicky I stated with manners. "Would you like orange juice or Kool-Aid?", she replied. Orange juice please, then I laid a couple grams of Kush on the table. Lexy was in the shower I heard water running from her bathroom. Ms. Vicky returned with orange juice and I pointed to the session for her to twist up. You were reading my mind Ahmir I haven't smoked one all morning she mentioned. Lexy came from the back room dressed in an Apple Bottom sweat suit. All I could eat was the eggs and one piece of toast my stomach was still aching. Lexy retrieved the plate and took it back into the kitchen. She returned then took a set on the sofa next me. Lexy tried consoling me while the three of us put a few dutches in rotation. There were a lot of rumors going around. Like Shanti was arrested because of me, I got caught cheating with my ex-girlfriend now I'm staying with some other girl. All kinds of mockery, but I didn't pay any mind. That just showed me how much people don't have to do with their time. After the smoke session I went and laid in the bedroom attempting to relax and enjoy the buzz. No one except my guy Red knew where I was so I felt safe for the moment. I phoned a few of my partners and we chopped it up about everything. They already knew what went down. See I'm so consistent with my ways and universal with the hustle tactics. That my street was through the roof. It only took one person to witness me doing one thing extra ordinary. Then the whole city would know it within twenty-four hours. This was potentially a drug bust with gorgeous women and some of the streets most potent Cali strain. Most definitely this was a trending topic and the talk of the town. Deep down everybody opinions and comments were only fuel to my fire. On the inside I was cut and sliced so sharply it was devastating. This was the most vicious blow I ever encountered in my 25 years of living. It wasn't about the, money it was the position the opportunity. Families were involved like I stated, I was feeding people and making a way for them. With my top f the line grade A sources and connections I was looking at the light. Who is to say those chances will ever present themselves again? Disappointment plagued my emotions most importantly my heart was involved. I couldn't recall ever having my heart crushed like this before.

Chapter 3

I demonstrated no signs of weakness. After discussing the terms with my partners, it was understood that the show must continue. Normally I would take the trip to Atlanta myself and get the product. For now, I must stand down and let my home boy's rock-n-roll. Just place my order and run my money then lay back. You can best believe when there is a will there is a way? The schedule would resume. I waited patiently for Ceasar to call me we needed to creep through the crib. I desperately needed to check for that loot I stashed. Something told me it was still there. I had $1,000 dollars each in two different pair of old pant pockets. Another $1,500 dollars in an old pair of old pair of jeans in the pant pocket. Folded neatly at the bottom of a basket of clothes in my bedroom. Even if they did raid the place, I had a gut feeling. That nine times out of ten they over looked the bread. It was noon when I received the call, I been waiting on from Ceasar. He informed me about his night and everything he witnessed upon coming home. I conversed with him about how everything happened so fast. I had to go for what I know and that's shake the scene. We live to fight another day the motto we live by. Even though things had gotten ugly overnight it would have to be one pill we had to swallow together. We decided t wait another day and get Joseph our pops to take us through there. Knowing that pops always up in the early morning hours everything should workout smoothly. We would park in the neighborhood behind our complex and enter the complex from behind. We still would have to enter the apartment through the front door. So, we have to be in and out like a robbery. Grab what we could then come on out quick fast and in a hurry. Hopefully the F.E.D.S wouldn't be watching. Even though they had no one in custody at the moment charges were most definitely going to be pressed. We just had to tread carefully and be patient until time reveals itself. You know them jump out boys play a dirty game. Ceasar even thought twice about continuing to work suspecting they would come for him. It was his name that was on the lease. Worst case scenario I would step and take the charge for the marijuana and paraphilia that was confiscated. The gun is registered to Cesar so they can't charge him with his own gun. An agreement was established between Ceasar and I we would follow up in the shining a.m. hours. We saluted one another then ended the call. After I stepped out back on the patio and called my fiancé. My patience was running out and I needed to see her. "Hey baby!" Shanti answered first ring on high alert. "How are you doing sweetheart? Are you ready to come get me?" I replied with a calm tone feeling like a champion. Knowing that I couldn't allow them to take me away from my love that easy. "Yes, baby! Where are you? I'm leaving now." Shanti responded with determination in her voice. I instructed her to a location that was a few blocks down from where I really was. Shanti was relieved then said she would be there in ten minutes. Lexy wasn't my woman so I owed her no explanation for my where about. I could come and go as I pleases. Lexy was so ecstatic that she was closer to me she felt she was winning. I would let her enjoy the shine for the moment because her spot was very convenient. No one would have ever thought I was there. While waiting for Shanti to arrive at the designated area. I called my mom and bribed her into letting me use her apartment for a couple of hours. My mom loved me so much, but she worried about me a lot because I was always into something. When it came down to it she knew I handled my business like a true gentleman. She gave into my request, but not before giving me strict instructions. First, she said she was only giving me a couple hours. Then she wanted me to burn some incense and leave her something to smoke. Today was her today off so she would be coming back to get in her bed. Relax and watch her stories until my dad got off work. I told her that her wish is my command. Leave the door unlocked for me because I would be there in thirty minutes. She agreed, then told me to be safe after saying out I love you and ended the call. My mom was a gangster herself so I didn't have to hide anything from her. Sometimes when we were together. We would put a dutch or two in the air go have a bite to eat and do our thing. My mom will smoke you under the table if you're a rookie. She a boss point blank period and it ran in my bloodline. Shanti pulled up in her silver 2012 Nissan Maxima which was low key and discreet from attention. What I like to call hater proof. Once I was in the passenger seat, we embraced each other with a long much needed juicy kiss. My eyes got watery, but I held back tears knowing this was a powerful moment and blessing. I could be sitting in a jail cell, but I'm here with my queen to be soaking up her love. We arrived at my mom's apartment, which was a middle class apartment. My mom always had a way of designing a relaxing décor and setting throughout her home. I noticed a sense of peace come over Shanti as she entered the living room I locked the door behind us and we passed through the small living room decorated with fancy furniture and live plants. My mother's apartment was nothing spectacular. Two bedrooms one bath. Shanti and I entered the extra room my parents basically for anyone who wanted to spend the night. I rolled a spliff then applied some clean sheets onto the floor not wanting to mess up the bed. After we smoked the spliff it was on Shanti and I got straight down to business. I had other plans for Shanti this go round. She will be getting all the treatment and the pleasure would truly be mines. We began kissing and caressing one another until we were butt naked. I laid her down on her back as she spread them long sexy legs wide as possible. My strong hands held her in position as I patiently kissed, licked, and sucked the juices from her throbbing vagina. She moaned out in ecstasy confirming that she was enjoying the triple threat pleasure my tongue was performing. She came multiple times before I bent her over. Kissing and licking her soft plumped cheeks all up in between her booty crack. Making sure it was dripping wet just how I like it. Shanti's body bucked as I penetrated her juice box from behind. With her head down and fine stallion backside arched to the ceiling. I went to work enjoying the site before my eyes as I hit it harder. Each time my long stroke would disappear deep inside her then reappear like magic. She screamed out from the pleasure of pain as I maintained control of her love cycle. Spanking her soft booty, pulling her long hair, and massaging her clitoris all at the same time. While whispering how much I loved her and how good she is to me. Shanti lost all control her vagina exploded milking my shaft with her juices. She screamed and moaned I love you Ahmir. With a high pitch sexy time over and over until I couldn't hold back any longer. Releasing my protein inside of her honey pot. She screamed and sighed oh yes give it to me daddy, give it all to mommy. I laid her flat down on her stomach whole still inside her juice box. Sweating and heavy breaths I could feel her walls grasping my manhood. Two hours passed by like a super charged Corvette. We had to get it together before my mom walked in on us. Shanti could barely move as we gathered ourselves trying to freshen up the best we could. Her body was still trembling from the love session we shared as I locked the door behind us on the way out. That was perfect timing I mentioned once inside the vehicle. A text message came through on my phone it was my mom and she said she was around the corner. I texted back informing her that we were gone and I did as she asked also. We cruised in silence whole I directed Shanti to run a couple errands then stopping to grab something to eat. While waiting in the drive-thru Shanti asked me why was I so aggressive with her this time? It was nothing like other time when we made passionate love in peace and harmony. It was more intensifying and exhilarating. Like I hadn't did it before or it would be my last time. Shanti pronounced looking into my eyes. I answered sweetheart that's the way I felt. I could be in jail ma so I had to remind you of what we have and share. I want you to always remember me for more than I am. I'm nothing like the average individual ma I have to expose you to your worth. With a man of my caliber in your world you will experience and fulfill feelings never imagined. It's only wise that you know your limits because we shall go the distance. Right or wrong sweetheart and that's how we living so believe that. "Ok daddy", Shanti said before kissing me on the lips. Shanti wasn't the nagging type she never questioned or disputed the things I told her. When I explained to her that I would be staying at my partner spot. In the projects where she picked me up from. Just for the time being until things cool down and I put a few more pieces back to the puzzle. She was cool with that long as she could call me and I was safe everything was fine with her. Before she dropped me off, we shared deep passionate kisses fondling each other private parts. She had my penis rock solid as she stoked wishing that I would be sleeping with her tonight. Trust me ma everything gone be alright I got it under control. I stated trying to ease her worries as she pulled off. She had to go get ready for work. She already took off today because of what happened the night before. I felt guilty lying to my fiancé about where I was staying. Survival is mandatory and I had to play the cards I was dealt. What she didn't know wouldn't hurt her plus in due time everything would reveal itself. By the time I made it back to Lexy crib Ceasar was calling and wanted to meet up. I instructed him on my where about then he came through for a couple hours. Ceasar stood almost six foot even stocky build brown skin and sometimes he rocked a beard. He the arrogant asshole type, but he was mindful and kept it one hundred at all times. Cesar wasn't my biological brother. His father Joseph which is my step dad and the man who raised me. Married my mom when we were kids like four or five years old. We grew up together Cesar and I was the same age, but he was a month older than me. My birthday was in October while his was in September. Over the years we grew closer together we shared some of the same dreams and hustles. We stood out on the patio conversing about the matter at hand. I put the flame to a freshly rolled Dutch and he popped the seal on two 24 oz Bud light Platinum's. We set the vibe as we contemplated on our next move. It was understood that we would be staying from house to house. Until we figured out what to do about the apartment. Deep down we both knew it was a matter of time before something jumped off. We didn't think it would be like this affecting us in ways we never imagined. Getting our pops to take us through the crib wouldn't be a problem so that would be our next move. I told Ceasar that I was gone keep rocking like cut off stockings regardless the circumstance. He stated that we should lawyer up and fight he case until the end. We brothers so we were gone ride or die regardless the circumstance. Ceasar and I kicked it for about two or three hours then he had to leave and go see Amari. He didn't break the news to her yet he just told her some foolishness jumped off, but didn't go into details. We gave each other dap then split. The next morning my pops and Ceasar pulled up on me ready to get this over with. We instructed pops to circle the neighborhood one good time by then we should be out. I was going to check for my cash only and Ceasar wanted to grab a few things. I couldn't believe my eyes them dirty cops trashed the place. Clothes and furniture were scattered everywhere. I was so disgusted that I didn't even bother to pick up any valuables my jewelry box was tossed around. They didn't take much, but they got the two-pound packages of Kush I had in the closet. They got Ceasar gun and some extra ammo to other weapons that weren't in the apartment. Fumbling through the clothes looking for the pants that concealed my cash. I found it all except $1,000 the cock suckers managed to find a stack a least they didn't get it all. My car was still out front they raided it pulling out the dashboard and C.D. player. Let's roll I said as Ceasar appeared from his room with a Gucci bag filled with items. You find it Ceasar asked? Yeah let's get on down we gotta get mom to come get all our stuff for us I replies. Bet that Ceasar responded then we were out just as quick as we entered. When we got back in the SUV with my pops, I phoned my mom. Informing he to get all of ur things for us a.s.a.p. and that I would pay her for it. They dropped me back off at Lexy crib then went on about their way we would meet up later. Once back in my comfort zone I counted my cash accumulating almost $7,000 wasn't a bad look. That's something I can work with I took $6,000 and cuffed it inside Lexy closet when she wasn't looking. Then I took the other $773 and put it in my pocket for other fees. I need to move around without being noticed so I called Rose to come get me. She mentioned that she wouldn't be free for another hour or two which was fine with me. Rose was my friend I'd known her since she was a young girl. With her mom being a close friend of the family over the years I watched her grow into the young woman she is now. She stood five feet five inches bright yellow skin complexion hazel brown eyes pretty pink lips She possess a pair of dimples in her cheeks that made her features drop dead gorgeous. She had been giving me the silent treatment lately because one day we had a disagreement and I accidently called her out her name. Ever since she heard about wat happened to me with the run in with the law, she's been cool. Plus, she knew I would do anything for her so she came through like she said she would. Rose drove a 2013 Hyundai Sonata which was super low key and hater proof. One day Rose was with me when I pulled up to serve Vicky and her friends. When she asked me where to come, I reminded her of that day. She remembered the location and said come on out she was already in the area. Mind you that this was the month of June middle of the summertime so the streets were blazing. I sported a pair of Ray Bans trying to conceal my identity and hopped in the ride with Rose. Like always she was looking beautiful as ever so that's the compliment she got when we embraced each other. I told her to clear her schedule for the day there were a few personal things I needed to take care of. She was cool with that so she let me drive and laid-back listening to her Beyoncé CD. First, I needed a fresh chop I wasn't feeling like my normal self. I just wanted to get back in the groove of things. I phone Chuckee to see if he could squeeze me in and he did just that. He didn't recognize the number so I had to call him twice. When he heard my voice, he was shocked because like everyone else he heard what happened. He told me he been blowing my phone up and it's just been ringing and no answer. I informed him to cut it out because I knew the police had my phone. Chuckee said come through a.s.a.p. his chair was open at the moment. I was already in the area so this would be snappy in and out like a drive-thru. Pulling into Mirror Cutz parking lot with Rose on the passenger seat reminded me of how sweet things just were. It was a Tuesday morning so business was slow when we entered the shop. It wasn't to many faces in the shop just the usual Drew and Mike. Drew had one in the chair and Mike looked as if he was doing some cleaning. Rose took a seat on the couch facing the fifty-inch flat screen T.V. monitor mounted on the wall. Chuckee just shook his head as we gave each other pounds. We chopped it up as he did his magic. After putting the final touches on the razor-sharp hair line. Chuckee wanted to know if I was holding any goods. I informed him that things were slow at the moment, but it would most definitely be this weekend. All I have is cash to pay you with today. I stated peeling off a twenty-dollar bill from my bank roll. Which is always good in this shop big bra money talks. Chucke responded as he spinned me around handing me a hand mirror and dusting hair from my neck and shoulders. I told Chuckee to lock that number in his phone and get at me this weekend on that tip. Then I gave him, Drew, and Mike dap before exiting the shop. Mike shouted! "Damn bra she with you?" As Rose got up to exit behind me. Holding the door for Rose I replied to Mike "It's not always the cards you were dealt, but how you playing your hand." Adjusting my Ray Bans and exited on that note. Once inside the Sonata Rose mentioned she was hungry and she didn't eat breakfast. Checking the clock, it was a little after ten and most places don't stop serving breakfast until 11:30 a.m. So, you still have time to catch the breakfast menu if you like I responded. "No, I'm ok I will be fine with some Chick-Fil-La.", she replied looking sexy as ever. I have to admit Rose was gorgeous and when the rays from the sunlight. Reflected off her hazel brown eyes and pretty skin it turned me on some serious. I didn't show any signs of desire I was content with what we shared. I already knew that if I wanted her in any type way, she would give me a green light. Rose was my friend and that's how I kept it. Turning the a.c. on blast to cool the car off. I put the car in reverse then navigated towards the northside of the city. Your hair cut looks really nice Ahmir he did a good job Rose commented with a smile on her face. Well, thank you Rose I appreciate the compliment. I replied. The waves must have been doing something to her because she kept looking my way as we rolled through the city. When we arrived at Chick-Fil-La I ordered me a hot meal also. After that we pulled into a Dollar General and finished up our food. I was in desperate need of some hygiene products. Once I had all of my hygiene in his buggy, I purchased a six ack of boxer briefs, ankle cut socks, and large t-shirts. I see a mini sports gym bag that I liked so I purchased that also then I was out. Down to my last spliff all I needed now was to score some Kush. Pulling into the Shell gas station I asked Rose if there was anything, she wanted to take care of. All se had to do was pick up some cash form this guy she mentioned. It was just now noon and I was in no rush to get back to Lexy crib. I peeled off a fifty0-dollar bill then told her to fill up on pump three and grab a box of mini swisher sweets. It looked safe so I pumped the gas as Rose returned from the store with the swishers and some snacks. Before pulling off I twisted my last spliff. Rose didn't smoke and she didn't like it when I smoked in her car, but she didn't trip this time. It was still some baby powder scent blunt killer spray in her console. From the last time I was in her car so we good I mentioned. On the route taking her to get the cash from some guy I phoned my boy L. I instructed him to put an ounce of Kush together for me and I'm coming to get it. Rose and I shared a few laughs. In the mean while I pulled oden on a couple more partners of mine updating them on my status and to kill some time. Shanti also called several times in between her lunch breaks, by this time it was pushing 5:00 p.m. in the evening and we had worked up an appetite. Rose and I ordered out from Logan's and that's when it happened.

Chapter 4

After Rose returned from inside Logan's with our food in hand. I couldn't even make it out of the parking lot before her phone rang. It was her God brother and he questioned her about me asking if we still conversed or not. Rose signaled for me to be quiet then she hit the speaker phone button so I could hear. Her God brother continued to speak. Is his name Davarious Scott? I heard him say. Yes, get to the point Rose emphasized. Well, they got him all on WBBJ News saying he's wanted in connection of a local drug bust. Also, they say he assaulted a police officer and is labeled a convicted felon possibly armed and dangerous. He then stated. Well, little sis I just wanted to verify if that was him or not maybe you can give him a heads up. Thank you for the information Eric. Rose said before ending the call. I couldn't believe what I just heard so Rose pulled it up on her Galaxy smart phone. There it was my description five o'clock news WBBJ T.V. West Tennessee. Looking in disbelief at all the charges they trying to put on me as I read on. Possession of marijuana with intent to resale, possession of firearm during commission of a dangerous felony. Assault on a police officer, evading arrest. Rose and I shook our heads as the news reporter went on with the bogus story labeling me armed and dangerous. My appetite immediately faded away and all I felt in my stomach was sickness. My phone started blowing up as I pulled out the parking lot. Ceasar, my mom, a couple of my partners all informing me of the same story. Not to mention Essence was blazing my hotline. I'd been trying to call her for the last two days and she had been sending me to voicemail even hanging up in my face. When I tried to call from my partner Bean phone, she clowned me. Ceasar and Bean just told me she blowing them up looking for me. Reason being the police just kicked her door off the hinges searching for me. I had a hard time processing everything the gates of hell just opened up for me. In need of some stress reliever badly so I pulled into a near store and twisted a dutch. Rose exchanged seats with me and I told her to drop me back off. Putting a flame to the medicated strain I tried gathering my thoughts as I took a pull from the aroma and inhaled deeply. Holding the smoke for several seconds then exhaling. Rose mentioned that everything would be okay and she would be there if I needed her. Taking that into consideration still I showed no signs of weakness. The show must continue even though my days were now numbered. We rolled in silence I just couldn't believe how they put everything on me. Rose dropped me off behind the projects that was across from Lexy house. I gave her a few extra dollars grabbed my things and thanked her. At that moment my mind kicked into grind mode and I was gone get it by any means. If those rotten cops wanted me, they would have to do their job I had no intentions on surrendering. Once back at Lexy crib I rolled up three more spliffs then laid across the bed and began to blaze. The weekend came quick and my partners Rello and Mac Key were ready to lock and load. We were getting high grade Cali bud from Atlanta for a little of nothing. Rello came through and I gave him $5,400. He was to return the next day with six pounds of the purest Cali bud on the streets where in Atlanta they called it gangsta. Any other time I would purchase ten or twenty pounds at a time. That would hold me for the week it all depends sometimes it wouldn't last no more than 72 hours. I just took a hit out of this world so six was all I could afford and I gambled on that. If anything went wrong on their end I would be struck. So, I prayed for my partners e had mouths to feed. We rocked like that for two weeks before the Feds ran in my guy Rello crib. They didn't get nothing off him just some paraphilia. They took him into custody and violated his two-year probation sentence he was on for a prior marijuana charge. That goes to show you the unjust system we up against, they arrest you for marijuana. Which is legal in many other states then send you to prison for it. It really doesn't make any sense if it's not one thing it's another. With Rello out of the picture I was forced to come out of hiding and get my hands wet. Mac Key didn't possess the skills it took to complete a mission like this on his own. Just like that I was back at it living that new Atlanta lifestyle all the rappers rap about. In my eyes it was ride or die, roll or get rolled on, you stack or starve and I had to get mines. Mac Key and I rock like that for about two or three weeks before his troubles came. The six and seven pounds we were getting a piece at a time weren't lasting 24 hours. One day we decided to take the trip to Atlanta on a week night. Arrive there early in the morning spend majority of the day there then come back home the following night. The whole ordeal was set up. I had just spoken to Mac Key. He stated that he was on his way to get me, but he never showed up. Come to find out he got pulled over leaving the compound. He had a half of ounce of Kush in his possession. The desperate officers took him in custody and violated his 11 month and 29 days probations he was on. It seemed as if everything we were building was falling apart now, I was on my own. It was too much for dissecting I didn't have any medication to ease the pain. Now here I was on the run from the law. Sitting out on my younger cousin Deseray balcony to come up with a solution. Lexy got to demanding so I gave up on her weeks after she threatened me for not having sex with her. I had to call my pops one evening. She got reckless with me because I stopped participating with her in sexual intercourse. Ever since then I been back and forth from hotel rooms and my cousin Deseray apartment. Deseray was 21 years old with a two-year-old some my little cousin J. She stood five foot five inches. One hundred twenty pounds with a petite frame. She bares the same light brown skin complexion as my sister and aunties. Deseray was the promiscuous type, but I truly feel she was just young and searching for guidance. That is what I tried to give her she always said she had true respect for me. Reason being I was her only boy cousin who didn't try to sleep with her. Deseray and I vibed she worked a day job and her son went to daycare every morning which was perfect for me. Sometimes I would stay gone all through the night then pop up on her early in the morning. When I knew she was getting ready to leave. Deseray loved my company one I was all about my cash two she was a smokeaholic. We had a fast gas session all day everyday that's all we did. I'm not gone lie I made her spot my own personal little candy store. It was already a very populated apartment complex. You could enter and exit from two different directions. The 45 Bypass and Hollywood Street which ran from one side of Jackson to the other. I was controlling traffic like a high school security guard. I had been on the run for about a month now plus I profited a little over $5,000 in that time. I got a little too comfortable at Deseray apartment which would soon be my downfall. Things were heating up and I could sense it. Sitting out on the balcony enjoying the evening summer time temperatures I contemplated on my next move. I was desperately in need of some strong cannabis my body grew accustomed to tit over the years. I was smoking more than I was eating which is a bad habit. Mac Key had the last of the Kush I was supposed to get half of what the police caught him with. Most importantly I needed to call the connect he was expecting us and now here it is more sad news. He didn't even know I was on the run I never told him because I didn't want him to feel itchy about me. I just mentioned some foolishness cracked off and I got jammed in the mix. He saluted that and never questioned me anymore about it. We just talked numbers not only were we consistent, but we came correct every time. If we owed him, we took care of it, if we miscalculated, we took care of that. It was vice versa with him. After contacting my boy L telling him to get an ounce of Kush for me. Knowing L, he would surely get it to me in a heartbeat. Once he gets it, he gone charge me a little extra for it and make him a profit. Which is cool with me as long as he gets it to me a.s.a.p. Then I dialed Choppo cell he answered after a couple rings. I explained what happened and that I couldn't make it that night. We would have to reschedule for the weekend he understood and was cool about it. Choppo was a millionaire and the cool calm collective type. He was never one of the many words. He was making a killing off us from Tennessee alone. I knew he hustled just to have play money and stay above the game. When we was linking up in Atlanta his whole squad were six figure guys or better. That's exactly what we were shooting for before all this madness took place. Now, that I had an understanding with the plug I was gone need a designated driver. That's when I started recruiting people that I caught a good vibe from and was already doing business with. The weekend was days away so I had to orchestrate something fast. First, was this quiet kid I met through Ceasar he had been shopping with me for a while. He was low key, and consistent and didn't speak much which told me he had some sense. Most importantly he drove a 2011 Chevy Impala all black with light tints, which was perfect for the highway. I text him to see if he was game for a trip to Atlanta. He had to check his work schedule then he said he was down for it. I didn't even know he had a job or his name which was law the less a person know the better. Of course, I would slice a few prices for him for providing the transportation. He actually did a great job he drove the whole way there and back nonstop except for gas and food. Something I never witnessed anyone do before. I have took this trip one thousand times and we always switch out to get some rest. This is a six hour drive from Jackson to Atlanta then another six hours back. That's a mandatory twelve hour trip because when we go get it we coming straight back with it. My guy really did impress me with his will power. He finished like a champion.

Chapter 5

We arrived at my cousin complex shared a victory dutch broke bread with one another then departed. It was time for some sleep the next day would be a busy one. I only copped eight pounds and they were going to the highest bidders. This flop will profit me $2,800 or better for the week it wasn't much, but I couldn't complain. Having to take matters into my own hands all the whole I continued to live the same lifestyle. Expensive weed and clothes, hotel suites, and champagne bottles. My aunt put a nice little shindig together for the 4th of July. I decided to take Shanti so she could meet more of my family and we can enjoy ourselves also. Shanti was a true soldier she stayed by my side the whole hundred yards. Shanti didn't miss a beat we made lover every chance we got and were taking trips at random. Gatlinburg, TN was a wonderful experience I could get use to the mountains and cabin lifestyle. 4/20 in Denver, Colorado was exclusive we boarded American Airlines to get there. They had some of the strongest cannabis strains I ever sampled. The only thing about that I couldn't enjoy the suite we were in, or the concerts we attended like I wanted to. Reason being the cannabis was too strong it kept putting me to sleep it truly was an amazing experience. Destin, Florida known for their white sand beaches that is one place I would have to visit again. You know what they say ball until you fall and Shanti and I were truly living in the moment. Up next was this local rapper by the name of Teezy. He did good business with me over the years so I helped him come up. We hollered at another partner of mine for a proper vehicle to ride the highway in. He came up with a Chrysler 200 for us which was low key and reliable. Teezy and I navigated out to Atlanta one calm summer evening. The plan was to get a room in Nashville and stay overnight then finish the trip the next morning. Everything was going steady even though I was on and off the highway at these awkward times. I still performed like a champion you know what they say it's hard to hit a moving target. We enjoyed the complimentary breakfast in the hotel room cafeteria before checking out. By the time we made it to Chattanooga it was still early and we needed to kill a few more hours. Atlanta Eastern Time is an hour ahead of TN western time so we pulled up into a cinema theatre and caught a movie. The Purge was some modern day Watts riot type of scenario. Teezy and I discussed as we exited the theatre ready to complete the mission. It was approximately $13,000 in my possession so whole we were burning time I gave Teezy half of it just to hold. $13,000 small bills look like a lot of money and created a bulge in my short pockets. Once back on the highway I started feeling agitated with the way Teezy was operating. He was too fidgety for me he was all amped up and excited about nothing. I mean we were trafficking in broad daylight plus I was on the run from Tennessee. Teezy was acting like a kid not to mention when we reached Atlanta. I looked over and seen him on Instagram recording and taking pictures with my cash. I just couldn't believe it, but I didn't even say anything. Little did he know this would be his first and last time taking a trip with me. I couldn't wait to catch my exit plus Atlanta traffic was busy and flowed perfectly. I sent a quick text to Choppo informing him that I would be arriving shortly. He was on command we pulled into the two story four car garage and handled business. It didn't take thirty minutes to vacuum seal wrap the packages roll a couple spliffs then departing back towards Tennessee. Navigating my way out of Atlanta I stayed in control of the wheel until I reached a low key exit outside of Nashville. Where I would allow Teezy to finish the trip and get a little rest. This would most definitely be the last time I deal with him. After this trip I was cutting his water off. At first I liked Teezy so I embraced him and helped him expand his hustle. I already knew him from around the city years prior. Plus, I never spent this much time around him to really feel him out. The whole time I was driving from Atlanta with over ten pounds of high grade marijuana on the back seat. This fool had the audacity to be trying to make a rap video. He was rhyming and rapping while recording on his phone plus his awareness was down. Unmarked cars state troopers were on high patrol and this fool was bouncing off the walls. Thank the Most High for my driving skills and tactics because that highway patrol was not match for my methods. We arrived in Jackson at our normal midnight hours. Teezy father was waiting in the complex for him. I was so ecstatic after all that the boy didn't buy nothing but one pound. I couldn't wait to get upstairs and give him his pound so he would be out my sight. My cousin was sleep I knew she would be getting up for work soon so I didn't disturb her. I twisted me a victory spliff and laid on the couch to get some rest. Before doing off I sent a quick text to Shanti, Choppo, and a few more cats informing them that everything was a green light. That's something I always did when I made it in town safe and sound. The next several days was one big party I had the candy shop jumping like Jordan. To be honest I got too comfortable at my cousin apartment and let one too many people figure out my location. Deseray promiscuous ways didn't make it any better. Some cat I was once feeding with a long handle spoon had a little thing with my cousin. He had a reputation for being a local snitch. It made sense because all the cases he caught he never did any time for them. Not to mention he swear up and down the two of us were cousins. Which was why I was feeding him with a long handles spoon in the first place. If it wasn't for the benefit of the doubt I wouldn't be dealing with him period. Ever since I been wanted by the cops I didn't make any contact with the boy. One hot summer day I was booming well out of Deseray's apartment while she was at work. That's when the fool called me talking about he got my number from Descray and he needed a half of pound. I went ahead and let him come through to get served. For some strange reason that was his last time contacting me. I didn't pay it any mind, but I did call Deseray. I had to remind her of the sour reputation the boy had. Then I told her not to be giving my number to anyone or telling people where I was. For the next couple of weeks I rocked solo and traveled in rental cars. I would go to Nashville at night and get a room. The following day I would wait around before going to Atlanta. Once I was in Atlanta I would hang out with Choppo for an hour or two then come to Tennessee. One morning I got in from Atlanta and I was really busy. Something was telling me to go get a room and clean the apartment. I guess I was just too smart for my own good. Always being under the influence impaired my judgement which only made matter worse. All the signs were clear enough for me to relocate real fast. For some reason I had to have been too relaxed in the candy store. That morning as I was pulling out of the complex. Headed to make a couple of drops and get a quick haircut. I noticed a cop car parked in the cut directly across the street. Thinking that I was too smooth in the low key rental car I continued to proceed in the opposite direction. Once I finished getting a haircut I net one of my partners at the store and got him straight. While I took care of business with my guy at the store. I noticed an unmarked church looking van with dark tints circling the parking lot of a nearby school. It was late August so school had been back in for a few weeks. I didn't pay the can any mind, but it did raise mu suspicion I kept it moving. Making a few more stops before heading towards Deseray's apartment. When I pulled into the complex I passed an all-black two door sport truck with dark tints. I could make out a figure in the car wearing a police looking uniform. Once again my alarm was triggered, but when the truck pulled off the thought faded away. The rental I was in made me feel secure because I knew no one seen me in it before that day. At least that's what I thought. At that moment my stomach was thinking for me. All the Kush smoke had my appetite on ten. So, I jumped out the rental went upstairs and warmed up some leftovers. It wasn't ten minutes before I heard beating at the door. U.S. Marshalls open up a voice screamed from the other side of the door. My heart dropped and my first instinct was run for the balcony side door. I tip-toed to the balcony attempting to make a run for my life. To my surprise the U.S. Marshalls had some company with them. Metro Narcotics had the complex surrounded and I had nowhere to run. They were aimed ready to fire with their barrels targeted at me. I ran back through the side door and the next thing I saw was the door fly open from the kick of the A.T.F officer. At least seven or eight A.T.F officers had their guns drawn. Demanding me to freeze and get down. Not wanting to get shot with no hesitation I dropped face down. All these cops in this apartment with me alone if I would have made any sudden moves. Then I would have been more than just another story for WBBJ News headlines. Without any resistance I surrendered and they cuffed me within a matter of seconds. As they searched the place for other suspects they saw an open bag concealing marijuana. They instantly raced out the door going to retain a search warrant. Now that my dooms day has surfaced. There were no questions that it was a jail cell with my name all over it.

THE END

Up next the revealing of spoken words

As we continue to build and contrive for the sake of our loved ones. We grow stronger through times of conflict and tribulations. The mind is a terrible organ to waste so we express ourselves with words of power. To make a connection with all readers is the goal that I'm after. If I may inspire one reader then mu journey is complete.

Words of Trending Topics

Bringing my thoughts into action a manifestation of pure satisfaction. My works are ecstatic flipping and rolling your body over like the gymnastics. I let go of bad habits because they led to situations that's drastic. Bouncing back like elastic, but I don't do magic. Some say I'm nasty cause I melt in your mouth right in the middle of traffic. Now, that's something to imagine. The feeling is oh so lovely mash potato smooth while chocolate covered. Multitalented I like it in the shower and kitchen. On top of the sheets or under the covers one position after another. I'm more than yo friend I can guide you like my distant lover. You don't have to worry my options vary. I'm the one who will get the job done so I get to it in a hurry. Staying consistent from the beginning I never changed, I just evolved into something that's more dependent. When I entered this game my only mission is to win it.

Words of Wisdom

Creativity is very necessary the world loves an articulate individual. Wisdom is the wise word spoken by the wise man. Wisdom is the manifestation of the foundation. Which is knowledge. Wisdom is symbolic to the heart which is the second main organ of the body that allows people to function. Cleanliness is next to Godliness so the heart must be kept with purity and righteousness. As a man thinketh in his heart he might as well manifested in his will. The heart must be aided properly so that it may produce accordingly. Intelligence attracts when you know and learn you can guide and teach. Structure must be established in order to operate productively. Understanding is the key to success. When you are acquainted with obstacles and circumstances you become capable of pursuing and conquering any battle. Fear nothing but the creator all of mankind was created equal. Knowledge, wisdom, understanding, and strength separates the ranks. Gods from men mortals from immortals. The strong may rule the weak, but the wise rule the strong. When faced with controversy and mixed emotions stand firm and maintain composure. Try not to panic or worry because it's necessary to become accustomed to battle as to daily labor. Struggles are very necessary true discipline is a reward from conflict. Growth and development comes from adversity when you know better you should do better.

Words of Refinement

Many worlds, nations, cultures, languages, personalities, formats, and motives with them all sharing one thing in common. These are some of the attributes and manifestation from the will of the Most High. The climates, environments, and communities have been established by the gifts that he share with the people and creatures of this life. As fish die when they are out of water so do people die without law and order. Proper structure and guidance will refine and civilize an individual. Without manners, respect, discipline, consideration, and self-control men and women are being made into beast form of wild life. Separating and departing without a cause. Envying and degrading one another while spreading slander and mockery about friends and family. Hatred, jealously, greed, and lust have destroyed humanity. There is no true value in the life that we lead in this day and time. These wicked traits are stronger than love, gratitude, admiration, probity, and sacrifice. These wicked traits destroy from within good character is opposed when sour and bitter energies overcome truth. To know your brother is to love your brother aid and assist him in the line of duty, battle, labor, even distress. There's always room for correction constructive criticism is need because it's a formula for growth and maturity. We as people of many nations must unite, build, and uplift and encourage out sisters and brothers. A foundation cannot be established without loyalty, unity, and respect at its finest.

Words of a Woman

To love her you must know her. When I say know her, I mean have a clear perception of her worth, history, and capabilities. To love her is to aid, assist, protect, respect, provide, guide, instruct and mold from within because a queen always come first and foremost. A king does not exist without a queen giving birth to his life. To love and know her is to grasp the meaning of understanding her essence of being and purpose of living. A woman's worth is held at a price that's nonnegotiable. A woman is a queen, she is the antidote. What she possess is sacred she herself is the secret chamber to the everlasting almighty, one and only all seeing most high.

The woman is symbolic to water reason being she gives the proper nutrients to yield and bring forth life. We must learn to respect and protect our women lifting them up to the highest degree. It's not about hookers in many skirts it's about getting a woman mind to work. Teach a woman what she may not know that will potentially refine and bring her in tuned with her worth. All women want to feel significant to a foundation. It's a woman's nature to love and comfort her man who in her eyes is superior on account of his strength and wisdom. With that being addressed it's only wise that we give our women the credibility she deserve. The authority to prevail and state her opinion on what should be and what is irrelevant. I know that a nation cannot rise and establish world peace until we first acknowledge our queens for who they are and properly orchestrate them with the correct teachings on what is predestined to be. A woman is everything she is the life giver, she is the head of this nation.

Word of Interest

Friends or lovers there will always be an aphrodisiac among us all. Temptation or tempted by sex appeal or a woman's beautiful features. The love cycle may build you up or break you down. When you share a strong affection with the opposite sex then you may love that person appropriately. Always analyze a situation acknowledge the pros and cons. Make sure there is compatibility between the two. Once a connection is established then you can build off of each other's energy. You become adequate to persist and move forward. Once a liaison is built you as lovers can share an experience of intimacy at its finest. No one is perfect, but there just may be someone perfect for you. Relationships doesn't come easy sacrifices must be made. Being optimistic is a important tool when dealing with mixed emotions and feelings. Knowing is one thing, but understanding is the key to happiness. Loving correctly will heal broken wounds. Some love harder than others so when you find true love be cautious not to take it for granted. It can be held at a value that's nonnegotiable satisfaction comes in many forms of communication and expressing your inner light will open doors to that sacred chamber. It's a woman essence to love and care for her king. Having intrinsic value for your queen can always be beneficial. With great quality demands even more quantity. There's no law against being spontaneous keep in mind no one deserve to live insatiable.

Words of Battle

Learning that it is necessary to become accustomed to battle as to daily labor. Nothing is brought into existence without hard work or controversy. Many struggles and difficulties are overcome with determination and confidence. You have to expect victory anyone can want something, but are you willing to put that 1,000 percent effort to get what you long for. Once you abate the doubt and fear you create power to persist accordingly. Your mental attitude must correspond with your endeavors. One must continue so that you can survive anything that you feel is contingent or that is not requisite must conclude. If it's not beneficial then it could potentially hinder you. To do away with aimless thinking and elevate into the ranks of scholars even Gods. One must learn to let your thoughts be for a purpose don't just let your mind wander and drift away aimlessly. Your thought process is the key to what makes you capable to pursue and endure any obstacles you may encounter. To be educated can consist of many different attributes. One can be in a state of awareness and consciousness which allows you to discern. One's perception should be substantial and evident. Structure is demanded hard work pays off abundantly and refinement is for all humanity. The highest form of intelligence shall be expressed at all times.

Words of Understanding

Let's agree to disagree my mistakes don't make. I refuse to let anyone actions worry me. I'm not perfect, but I'm destined to be. Pay attention closely correct me if you feel it's necessary. I can't be anything lesser than the gentleman that I am. Even when no one is watching I carry myself like a man. I'm not arrogant I'm educated I know better so I do better any man that chooses his battles wisely is very clever. I'm open-minded and patient there is nothing about me basic. Simple things are extra ordinary materialism is very temporary. Each one teach one stand up not out the strong way never the wrong way. Play chess not checkers or don't even get involved. Constructive criticism is needed there's not a woman alive that deserves to be mistreated. Love her, guide her, comfort her, support her, protect her, but most importantly keep her first. Don't entertain foolishness stay away from negativity. Be yourself never pretend to be something you're not. Let you woman features fulfill you allow the Most High blessings to heal you. Be cautious of whom or what you choose to do. Be self-observant meditate on what you're learning. When the going gets tough go harder when life beats you up think smarter. Practice makes perfect accomplish it if you feel you deserve it. Know your worth and last but not least no matter what you pursue or where it may lead never forget where you come from.

Words of Praise

Requesting forgiveness for all my sins and faults. Searching for strength to make it through my battles. In need for guidance to a path that's much straighter. Giving praise and thanks to the Most High for allowing me to prevail this far and letting me witness the sun. I give praise to the Most High for building himself up from nothing then sharing his power with me. All praise is due to the Most High for sending his messengers and blessing with knowledge and understanding to know his truth. Continuing to plead for forgiveness for my faults I could never be perfect. I'm only here to enjoy my stay while spreading peace among the people. Speaking truth for the people that are willing to listen. The more I make mistakes the more I'm gathered towards the Lord. Mistakes are getting old and time waits for no man. I'm only mortal but my immortality appears in different forms. Only one with wisdom will understand your mind has to be open to truth and knowledge of self. All praise is due to the Most High for allowing me to live again I'm no longer astray. Asking for correction and forgiveness sometimes I get the feeling as if I ask for too much. So I'm thankful and grateful knowing you have truly blessed me.

Words of Attributes

Sweet victory I'm chasing my destiny the hunt is always better when your Queen is just as hungry. How sweet word of sincerity can heal and aid wounds that have been scared so deeply. We may face some difficulties unfolding out mysterious and researching our history, but that's real chemistry. You believe in me I believe in you. Your loyalty is all I need to make my dreams come true. While traveling on this road tell me who wants to be alone? Sometimes my heart aches and I need a shoulder to lean on. My mother gave birth to a lover not a fighter I speak my soul through the wire. While praying for a better way and waiting for better days. I take heed of the message and I'm no longer astray. Majority of the time I listen with more than my ears. Some say I'm gifted because once in my presence you can feel my tempting energy. I'm heating up to the third degree it's hard to breathe in my section. I'm itching for perfection I'm the rest area for all pedestrians. Welcoming all challengers I'm T.K.O in the first round and still standing like stamina. Twenty four hours plus come get you a rush. I got women bodies soaking wet dripping sweat as if I was teaching swim lessons. Addicted to the bobble head woman love the way I play it especially when I bust. This for the grown up's no minors I'm chopping this lesson up for free and these are coaching strategies for all amateurs. If you feel the need then I'll balance you I am the equation come figure me out I'm patiently waiting.

Words of Confinement

Who ever thought it would come to this, just where did I go wrong? Praying night and day accepting responsibilities for my actions as a man. Now, I'm leaving everything in God's hands wondering what happened to my master plan. I warned them of what would happen, but they didn't listen. Now that it all has fallen down look like I'm the victim I've been victimized. Who am I gone call now is the question? I know many are pleased that my troubles have surfaced. Making a mockery of me like I can't put these pieces back to the puzzle. See now I know you can run you can hide you can plot you can plan, but Karma has demand. Be wise when you play your hand because time waits for no man. Confined to a isolated area over populated with many types of predators. My mind is open my thoughts are free I can see through what's in front of me clean across the Arabian Sea. My senses triggered my heart craves for knowledge and sources. As I listen all I hear is negativity coming from strange voices. Forced to feed off my own positive energy focused on growth and development spiritually. Now this is my higher power working at it's finest. He's in fill control over what happens next so I'm praying for guidance. The devil is busy, but I'm not surprised I refuse to fold I refuse to cry. My thoughts are traveling faster than the speed of light. My mind searches for something in common. My heart is beating while my blood is pumping. Where this may lead? I may not know, but my laces are tied and i'm ready to go.

The Art of Poet Philosopher

With so many pictures painted in these short series of events. Who is to say what levels we may exceed? Through consciousness and renewal of the mind the sky is the limit. This auto biography is very unique and one of a kind. It contains three different tall tales which are based on a true story and corresponds with on main topic. Each short story leads up to the revealing of three different formats of writing. Which are philosophies, poetry, and spoken words. Each short story shares a symbolic meaning for a way of life that is corrupted. No matter how many times you try to do illegitimate things differently. You always get the same results destruction. The only true solution is change completely and a way of life that's righteous. Ahmir is the main character used in this story that this bio is based on Philosopher is the title chose by the author himself, which is meant to inspire all readers.